THE BILTMORE'S *MONA LISA*

A Heist Novel

Daniel D. Smith, Sr.

The Biltmore's Mona Lisa. Copyright © 2024 by Daniel Dee Smith, Sr.

All rights reserved. No part of this book may be reproduced, stored in a retrieval system, or transmitted by any means, electronic, mechanical, image copied, recorded, or any other means of usage without written permission from the author. NO AI TRAINING: Without in any way limiting the author's exclusive rights under copyright, any use of this publication to "train" generative artificial intelligence (AI) technologies to generate text is expressly prohibited. The author reserves all rights to license this work for generative AI training and development of machine learning language models. The name and trademark of the above copyright holder may be used in advertising or publicity pertaining to this work without written prior permission. Title to copyright in this work and any associated documentation will always remain with the copyright holder.

Cover design by Daniel D. Smith, Jr.

This is a work of fiction. Names, characters, places, and incidents either are the product of the author's imagination or are used fictitiously, and any resemblance to actual persons, living or dead, businesses, companies, events, or locales is entirely coincidental.

Smith, Daniel Dee, 1944-
The Biltmore's Mona Lisa

Library of Congress Control Number 2024909760 (print)
ISBN: 979-8-9905843-0-3 (hardbound)
ISBN: 979-8-218-37483-9 (paperbound)
ISBN: 979-8-99005843-1-0 (eBook)

Published by the author
DanielSmithBooks.net
Chattanooga, Tennessee
Printed in the USA
9 8 7 6 5 4 3 2

For Betty, Angela and Daniel

THE BILTMORE'S
MONA LISA

"Thou shalt not covet…"

— *Exodus 20:17*

PROLOGUE

At the World's Fair in New York City in 1939, the French government displayed a national treasure, Leonardo da Vinci's world-renowned *Mona Lisa*.
As the Fair ended, the Germans were threatening war and invasion. The French government debated bringing the famed painting back to Paris. In Paris, the Louvre was already planning to move its most valuable works to the South of France.

The Roosevelt administration offered to house the *Mona Lisa* in the Mellon Foundation's collection until the new National Gallery in Washington opened. The French accepted. Two curators and two Paris policemen remained in the U.S. to ensure the painting's safety.

The painting was hung at the National Gallery in Washington, DC, when it opened in March 1941. After Gallery senior curator Daniel Roberts conducted a detailed study, the Gallery erected a display next to the painting, recounting its history.

The painting was finished around 1507, although some historians believe da Vinci continued to work on it, tinkering with it off and on through 1517. The Italians called the painting *La Gioconda*. In France, her name is *La Jaconde*. The subject in the painting is believed to be Lisa

Gherardini. 'Mona' is a contraction of 'Ma Donna (My Lady).' So, in English, we have the *Mona Lisa*. The *Mona Lisa* was Leonardo's favorite painting. He did not want to let it go and considered it unfinished. The French king, Francis I, purchased her from Leonardo just before his death or from Leonardo's assistant soon after Leonardo's death in 1519. After the French Revolution and after Bonaparte had displayed the painting for four years, it was moved to the Louvre Museum in 1804. The work introduced many new painting and modeling techniques, such as the lack of jewelry or other adornments. Up to that time, all paintings showed elaborate adornment on the subject. Leonardo did not follow the usual posing in portraits, which, until then, had the subject stiff and upright. Leonardo had Lisa Gherardina sitting in a relaxed manner. The painting was done in oil on a piece of poplar wood. It's small for a famed piece, only 30" high by 20" wide. Also noted on the display was that the *Mona Lisa's* poplar wood panel had been stabilized on the reverse to stop the panel's warping, which had worsened over the years. It mentioned that the frame had been changed at least four times since its original painting. This was primarily due to changes in taste over the centuries. In 1909, a well-known collector, the Comtesse de Behague, gave the painting its current frame, a Renaissance-era work consistent with when the *Mona Lisa* was painted.

In 1911, she was stolen by a part-time employee of the Louvre, an Italian named Vincenzo Peruggia, and was missing for a little over two years. During the two years the painting was missing, a master art-forger named Yves Chaudron made six exact copies. Chaudron planned to sell his copies, presenting each as the original to wealthy private collectors. When asked, Peruggia did not know who Chaudron commissioned to recreate the frames. When she was returned to the Louvre, a rumor spread that the Chaudron copies were of such exceptional quality that the returned painting was one of the replicas.

Many feared the ongoing European war would eventually draw in the United States. In 1941, Raymond J. Rogers, curator of the National Gallery and a veteran of the Great War, remembered the penetration of German submarines into U.S. coastal waters. He suggested to board members that they move a selection of the best artworks from Washington to a safer place in the interior.

The selection team, comprised of the Gallery's R.J. Rogers, U.S. Senator Archibald Wellington, and U.S. Representative Madolyn Rockefeller, chose the Vanderbilt estate in the mountains of North Carolina. The committee sent head curator Raymond J. Rogers to get approval from Cornelia Vanderbilt Cecil and her husband, John.

On August 8, 1941, without fanfare, they shipped two moving van loads of artwork to Asheville. Among the paintings were the French government's *Mona Lisa* and works by Rembrandt, Raphael, Goya, and Vermeer.

The paintings were accompanied by Daniel Roberts, a senior curator at the Gallery, two French curators, and two French policemen.

With the works stored in two large connecting bedrooms on the second floor of the Biltmore House, Roberts, the Frenchmen, and a small contingent of North Carolina Highway Patrolmen guarded the priceless collection around the clock.

Daniel D. Smith Sr.

BOOK I:
THE GERMANS

ONE

BILTMORE HOUSE
OUTSIDE ASHEVILLE, NORTH CAROLINA
AUGUST 11, 1941

Antoine Buchard stood in the cobblestone drive before the great house, shivering in a light topcoat on an unusually cool August day. Buchard, a short, slim, academic-looking gentleman, sported a thick mustache and wore round spectacles. A fastidious dresser, he favored bowler hats and sported an elaborate watch fob presented to him by the director of the Louvre.

Buchard needed to choose suitable rooms to store the priceless paintings. The two Allied Van Lines trucks, full of artwork, had just arrived. Daniel Roberts, the lone curator from the National Gallery, had requested that Buchard select the safest rooms for storing the 82 pieces of invaluable artwork.

After being briefly introduced to Cornelia Vanderbilt Cecil and her husband, John, Buchard excused himself to survey the second and third floors. Initially, he'd considered storing the artwork and housing the security team at the basement level. However, because of the indoor swimming pool, there was a higher risk of condensation, with potential mold and mildew. The security team had to remain near the artwork, so the basement would not work for them either.

Not wanting to hold the trucks up any longer than necessary, he made a speedy 20-minute inspection of all the rooms. While glancing at the Damask Room, Buchard thought even the wallcoverings were a work of art. Ruling out the rooms that John Cecil, Cornelia, and their two sons occupied on the second and third floors left Antoine with the choice of the left wing of the second floor or the left wing of the third floor. Buchard chose the second floor.

Not wishing to use the elevators at the far-right end of the house, Buchard decided to have the artwork, which included seventeen sculpture pieces, carried up only one flight of stairs instead of two. As Buchard and Daniel Roberts directed, the French policemen, Maurice and Jules, and three movers struggled to carry the larger pieces up the one flight of stairs. At the first curve in the stairway, three movers dropped the corner of the large crate carrying Botticelli's *The Adoration of the Magi*. A quick inspection found that only the outer packing case had suffered some damage.

Roberts directed the seventeen sculpture pieces to be placed in the Tyrolean Chimney Room, while Buchard directed the crated paintings to be placed in the Louis XV Room.

It took three men to carry most of the sculpture pieces, and it would have likely not been possible if the Biltmore staircases had not been more expansive than a standard staircase. Even with the challenging weight loads, the job only took three hours.

Buchard chose the corner Damask Room as his sleeping quarters so he could be close to the artwork. Roberts would sleep in the Sheraton Room. The two policemen would share the Old English Room. His assistant, Phillipe Jourdan, would be in the Claude Room. Phillipe's room had no bath, so he would have to use the one in the hallway.

Antoine thought it interesting that Cornelia Vanderbilt Cecil's suite and the room where their two sons slept were on the third floor, while John Cecil's bedroom was on the second.

Antoine had set up watch shifts of twelve hours on and twelve hours off. Two men would be on watch around the clock in the rooms with the artwork.

Even though the American curator was technically in charge of all the paintings from the National Gallery, Buchard hadn't initially included him in the watch roster, believing Roberts would rather spend most of his time associating with the Cecils. Roberts reminded him of what an academic professor would look like. Roberts was tall, slim, and fit, always wearing a tweed sports coat with elbow patches and a sweater that showed a shirt with a collar over the sweater. He frequently smoked a pipe.

But when Roberts heard he wasn't on the rotation, he raised such a fuss that Buchard had made a particular slot for him as a "supervisor" from 10 a.m. to 4 p.m. This addition to the schedule would allow the Frenchmen to eat a hot lunch in the room by the service entry, catered by the Biltmore staff. Roberts seemed relieved when Buchard told him of the schedule change.

The Gallery had alerted Raleigh of the artwork's arrival. As a result, the state assigned three highway patrol cars with two troopers in each for security. They stood eight-hour shifts around the clock, stationing their vehicles in the stable's courtyard. One patrolman was to patrol the outside grounds once every hour. The stable's courtyard was connected to the carriage house, the carpenter's shop, and the main service entrance. To avoid entering the house, the patrolmen used the restroom in the large stables close to where they parked their vehicles. They brought sandwiches and thermoses. They skipped the walking rounds when the weather was rough until it improved.

The Gallery offered to pay for the meals for the museum personnel, but the Cecils would not accept it. Beyond the kitchen were two pre-delivery rooms, the delivery entrance, and the stable's courtyard, where the highway patrol car parked.

Antoine, Phillipe, Maurice, Jules, and sometimes Roberts ate in the room just off the kitchen courtyard. When they finished, they returned to the third floor with food for the watch, which had remained with the artworks. Daniel Roberts often stayed with the artworks while the Frenchmen ate together.

THE WHITE HOUSE OVAL OFFICE
WASHINGTON, D.C.
AUGUST 18, 1941

"Mr. President, Prime Minister King is here."

"Send him in, Grace."

William Lyon Mackenzie King, the Canadian Prime Minister, strolled into the well-known room.

Franklin Delano Roosevelt rolled his chair around to shake his friend's hand. His military attaché stood behind him. "Welcome, Mac. Your assistant didn't tell us what you wanted. Is this about your war efforts or your ambitious ship-building program?"

"In a way, Franklin. While we've been transporting our troops to England to assist the British, Winston has asked us to fill our returning ships with German and Italian POWs. He says England's camps are full, and there is nowhere to build more. Now, our three camps are full, and the Canadian people aren't up to us building more at this time. It will take a while for me to sell them. In the meantime, I've got a shipload arriving in two days."

"That is a problem, Mac. What's that got to do with us?"

"I've come to ask you to take some of our POWs, Franklin."

Franklin puffed on his cigarette. "Mac, my people overwhelmingly want to stay neutral in all this. They wouldn't go for that. We're not at war with anyone."

"Franklin, I'm desperate. I'm pleading for you to help out here. Let me suggest this: my arriving shipload of POWs consists of a hundred officers. Mostly Kriegsmarine, with a few Luftwaffe officers. I'd think the American people would be less opposed to the civilized officer corps than to camps full of enlisted POWs. Would you, at least, take these hundred officers? I'm down to begging you, Franklin."

Commander Alistar Knox, the president's naval attaché, leaned over and whispered into the president's ear, "Sir, we have one existing Great War POW camp that has been restored and is currently being used as a tourist attraction. It is fully functional. It's located in remote Crossville, Tennessee."

The president puffed, pensively blew a smoke ring, and said, "I'll likely live to regret this, but, okay, Mac, we'll take your hundred German officers. I insist on bringing in the International Red Cross; otherwise, we'll try to keep this hush-hush. I'll blame any extra heat on you, somehow. If we get a lot of pushback, I'll sell it as a humanitarian move. You store them someplace for a week, and we'll get supplies and personnel assigned to Camp Crossville. Then you can transport them down."

JAGEMANN'S ART GALLERY
FIFTH AVENUE, NEW YORK CITY
SEPTEMBER 6, 1941

Lillian Jagemann, in her forties, tall, blond, and sturdy, was in her office unusually early on a windy September morning. Her young assistant, Darla Patton, usually arrived a couple of hours after her.

Lillian flipped through the morning's mail. She paused at an envelope from her sister. She'd not heard from Elise in over a year. Their parents divorced when they were teenagers. Elise had gone with her mother, who chose to use her maiden name when she moved down South, and Lillian had stayed in New Jersey with her father.

Now, Elise worked as a maid at the Biltmore estate outside Asheville, North Carolina. Lillian had once visited her on an art-purchasing trip to Atlanta and New Orleans.

Dear Sister,

I hope this finds you well. Aside from my knees killing me from going up and down the many stairs here, I'm doing fine.

Since you deal with artwork, I thought you would find my latest news fascinating. The National Gallery in Washington, D.C., has just delivered two truckloads of masterpieces to the Estate for "safe keeping."

Staff members say it includes da Vinci's Mona Lisa! However, I don't know for sure since we're not allowed in that part of the house until background checks are completed.

A team of Frenchmen came with the artwork. Rumor has it there are two curators and two plain-clothes cops. The state police constantly patrol outside. The Frenchmen sometimes eat with the staff, and I heard one mention the Alba Madonna. That sounds like artwork to me.

You'd find all this fascinating, I bet. I hope you can come to visit again!

Much love, as always,

Your sister, Elise.

Lillian leaned back and stared out the window at the ever-present flow of office workers, tourists, and passing taxi cabs.

Lillian's family had immigrated when she and her sister were young, but she was German at heart, much more so than her sister. Lillian was the oldest by three years and had more fond memories of Bremerhaven than her sister.

Before the rumors of war had grown, she'd found and purchased two lovely old masterpieces for a German client, Hermann Goring, in the late 1920s. These days, Goring was Germany's second most powerful man, behind Adolf Hitler. Goring loved the old masters and enjoyed artists that Lillian had heard Hitler despised. Bruno Lohse, one of Goring's primary art brokers, had handled the deal. She'd promised to inform Lohse if she ever came across something else, especially a collectible.

Even while it would never be for sale, what could be more interesting than da Vinci's *Mona Lisa*? thought Lillian.

The German consulate would not consider passing on any correspondence Lillian might write to Bruno Lohse. But surely, they'd forward anything to Reichsmarschall Hermann Goring. She would write and let Goring know this exciting story from Elise.

Lillian had an acquaintance at the Consulate. She picked up the phone, but, having second thoughts, she decided to get a letter to Goring covertly. She would ask her Consulate acquaintance, Karl Gernhardt, to send a letter within a letter. Her first letter was to Karl. Her second letter included the complete story.

Considering the escalating tensions between Germany, Italy, and the United States, Lillian guessed that the FBI would monitor the Consulate. So, when her assistant, Darla Patton, came into work, Lillian instructed her to hand-deliver the letter to Karl Gernhardt at the Consulate's front desk.

Slim and lovely Darla had often been told she was a dead ringer for actress Betty Grable. She walked the four blocks and entered the gated compound. After leaving her envelope, she returned to the gallery.

With that completed, Lillian went back to running a failing gallery. The Depression had been terrible for sales. The only things that helped her were her husband's inheritance and her own skill at purchasing artwork for a fraction of its value during the Depression. Now, with war likely approaching, sales were down again. In fact, she was overdue on her lease. Was there possibly a way she could profit from this new information?

ARMY AIR CORPS MOTOR POOL
RANDOLPH FIELD, SAN ANTONIO, TEXAS
SEPTEMBER 6, 1941

Lieutenant Declan Donahue's office was a shack in the corner of the vast motor pool garage. It measured eight feet by ten feet and barely held a desk, three chairs, and a filing cabinet. In addition to the door, one four-pane window looked into the maintenance area.

A badly mangled steel propeller from a Vultee BT-13A trainer was propped up in one corner.

Donahue was at his desk, trying to block out the hammering and motor sounds from the maintenance work outside. He leafed through maintenance reports, approved vehicle request forms, and checked scheduled gasoline deliveries. A far cry from a flying career, he thought.

His gaze fell upon the propeller. After serving as an infantry officer for five years, he'd volunteered for Air Corps training, hoping it would offer faster promotion. Advancements for infantry officers had been non-existent. He was still a first lieutenant after being in the Army for eight years.

After being accepted for flight training and transferring to Randolph Field in Texas, Donahue completed the first part of his training and was ready to do his first solo. Immediately upon taking off, though, his engine failed. Half a mile from the runway's end, he crashed into a grove of pine trees.

He'd lost his left arm and had broken both legs. After months in the hospital and more months of physical therapy with a fitted prosthesis, the Army wanted to retire him on disability. Since he wanted to stay, he'd pleaded his case before a review board. He'd listed his experience and the Army's investment in him. No doubt, bearing in mind the pending conflict in Europe and Japan's aggressive moves in the Pacific, the board agreed on a one-year trial period, placing him in charge of the motor pool at Randolph Field. That year had come and gone. He'd heard nothing more from the Army and was even on the latest list for promotion to captain.

On his desk was a small Chinese puzzle box. He picked it up and began working its sixteen opening sequences. Doing this was more difficult, considering his prosthesis. He used his artificial hand to push down on the top of the box to hold it in place while he opened each sequence with his right hand. He often fiddled with the box when he wanted to relieve stress or to relax.

The motor pool's master sergeant banged the door open, bringing more noise and a smell of gasoline into the office. He sat in one of the two available chairs. "Got the scheduled gas deliveries, sir?"

Donahue handed him the report. "Anything going on I should be aware of, Sergeant?"

"No, sir. This here pool runs on her own." Noticing the puzzle box in Donahue's hand, he said, "What's the story on that box, Cap?"

Donahue pushed it closer to the sergeant. "It's a souvenir from my service in China in the early 30s. I've researched them. The puzzle boxes are believed to have been started in the early 1800s. Initially, they were functional; an inner compartment was used to hide valuables, such as jewelry or money. Later, they mostly became tourist trinkets."

The sergeant said, "That's really interesting. I think I'll try to find one for Ben. Say, you want a car to take a drive?"

"No thanks, I've got to finish these other reports. Why don't you take the rest of the day off? Surprise your wife. Take Ben out of school early and go fishing."

"Thanks, Lieutenant."

The sergeant departed.

He used the eraser end of a pencil to scratch at the point where his prosthesis was attached to his stump. This was a frequent problem. It often woke him up at night. He didn't believe it would ever go away.

His thoughts drifted to his dates with Alaina Avara, the physical therapist who had worked with him through his many months of therapy with his prosthetic arm. Alana had been transferred to South Plains Army Air Field in Lubbock. They'd gone out to dinner twice, and he felt there was a growing connection between them. Then, she'd been transferred. He had not seen her in more than six months. They had written, but the letters were becoming less frequent. He did miss her. He'd like to know if she missed him too, or was it turning into a one-way relationship? She'd be at work now. He'd try to call her tonight.

TWO

AIR MINISTRY
WILHELMSTRASSE, BERLIN
OCTOBER 12, 1941

The mid-October weather defied normal patterns with its dryness and unseasonable warmth. Military vehicles filled the wide Wilhelmstrasse.

Lieutenant Rolf Gunther stood sweating in his greatcoat, looking up at the gigantic German Air Ministry building. Rolf was not a Luftwaffe pilot; he had spent two years as an infantry officer before transferring to the Air Force intelligence branch. At just under two meters tall, Rolf was taller than most Germans. With his brown hair and brown eyes, he was not the picture of pure Nordic look that Nazi ideology desired. But, then, Rolf had never joined the party, either.

He'd been to the Air Ministry only twice before. Gunther had met Reichsmarschall Goring, commander-in-chief of the German Air Force, after he and his father returned from Dearborn, Michigan, in 1933. On that trip, they'd been visiting Henry Ford and discussing Gunther Senior's automobile business in Berlin.

Today, he was here because Goring had summoned him. Goring's secretary had said only that the Reichsmarschall would reveal further details when he arrived.

Entering the reception area, Gunther quickly crossed the highly polished, elaborate marble floor. A receptionist greeted him at a counter that reminded him of the Adlon Hotel's check-in desk. A female sergeant told Gunther they expected him and instructed him to accompany a private standing next to the counter area.

They climbed two flights of massive marble stairs, then turned left and entered Goring's outer office. This area had wide, polished wooden parquet floors with intricate designs, a gorgeous crystal chandelier, and a dusty painting encased in an elaborate frame. Directed lights illuminated it. Another, very attractive female sergeant in Luftwaffe blues occupied an elaborate table desk. "Have a seat, sir," she said. "The Marshal will call you shortly."

As he admired the large carved double wooden doors, which he assumed would lead into the inner office, the sergeant said, "The Reichsmarschall will see you now, sir."

Entering Goring's inner office, Gunther, who had thought the outer office was grand, now saw two elegant multi-tiered crystal chandeliers, two large leather couches, and a coffee table upon which three interesting ashtrays and a large crystal lighter sat. One ashtray was a zeppelin airship attached to a docking tower, another was a WWI Fokker-D flying over an ashtray base; it looked to be WWI trench art, and the third was a hand-carved crystal ashtray with a reclining nude motif. Against the righthand wall sat a carved minibar stocked with a silver ice bucket and crystal glasses, along with bottles of Schnapps,

Russian vodka, and what appeared to be scotch whisky. Twelve to fifteen lavishly framed Rococo and Baroque-style paintings were hung around all four walls. He also saw a gigantic carved teak desk, a sizeable sepia painting of the Fuhrer, a map of England and the French coast, and a sizeable global atlas encased by an intricate hand-carved atlas stand sporting a King Neptune motif.

With measured steps befitting his military background, Goring strode from around his desk to shake hands. "Ah, Lieutenant Gunther."

Gunther took in the General's custom-made uniform, which sported Germany's highest military award from the Great War, the Pour le Merite, informally called the Blue Max. Goring also wore the Iron Cross first class and several ribbons from the Great War. Goring had received these awards for his service as a high-scoring Luftwaffe pilot in the previous war.

The General led him to a portrait painting and said, "Isn't this a wonderful piece?"

Gunther did a double take, "Herr Reichsmarschall, isn't that the famous Mona Lisa?"

"It is, Gunther! More correctly, it's a copy by a French art-forger, completed around 1912. I acquired it in 1920. I enjoy it, but I'd love to own the original. How's your father and mother?" Goring went on, turning from the painting, "It saddened me to hear of the loss of your brother."

"Not well, sir. Mother passed away last year from pneumonia. Father lost his business four years ago. The automobile business died during the non-military-related economic downturn over the last eight or nine years. He's also now in poor health."

"I'm sorry to hear all that. Please tell Frederic I asked about him. Let my staff know if we can do anything to help with your father's care."

"Thank you, sir, I'll tell him."

"Would you like something to drink?"

"Sir, I'm sure you're busy."

"Rolf, how do you think our war effort is going?"

After a moment of reflection, Gunther replied, "If I can be frank, sir, I believe it's going very well, but the U.S. may enter the war soon. Since I've been to America a few times, I think it might be wise to be concerned about their ability to ramp up the production of aircraft and other war materials."

"Even if the U.S. enters the war, they can't present much of a challenge for at least eighteen months. Russia will have surrendered by then, and we'll finally be free to take England down. After all that, America will cower and collapse in view of our might."

"I have little knowledge about that, sir."

The Marschall looked at the da Vinci copy again. "I mentioned I have a unique project. You could be a great asset."

"I'd be honored to do whatever I can, Herr Reichsmarschall."

"As you may have heard, I have many cultural interests. I've been informed that someone moved a painting I'm concerned with into a location where I may be able to access it. I want to send a small team to the United States, to North Carolina, to be specific. I plan to steal the real Mona Lisa from an estate near Asheville. I want to present the painting to *Der Fuhrer* for his planned Fuhrermuseum. I'd like you to plan the operation, choose the team, and provide me with a solid plan, a timeline, and the team members' backgrounds. Would you accept that assignment, Rolf?"

"Sir, I'm uncertain I'm the best person to do this. However, I'd do anything you asked. I'll try to devise a workable plan."

"I've read your record, Rolf. You have infantry tactics training, leadership training, and intelligence-gathering training. You're more than qualified."

"As you wish, General."

"Excellent, Rolf. Now, this building has hundreds of rooms. Pick one for your office during this planning stage and let Sergeant Reicher, the blonde out front, know what else you might need. Your budget will be generous, let us say. General Weiss will be your senior reporting officer, but I want to know all the details. I'll issue orders so you'll encounter no obstacle to what you need for this assignment."

"Yes, sir. I'll do my best."

Standing in the lobby, Rolf slowed his breathing. He wondered; Can I write a plan to do this? How do I get to America? Is this even doable?

Giving himself time to collect his thoughts, he decided to walk the fifteen blocks back to his hotel room.

* * *

Back at the Ministry the following day, Gunther located a small room on the third floor. Leaving his bags there, he asked Reicher to move in a table that would hold up to six, a large map of the Southeastern United States, six chairs, a filing cabinet, and two lamps. He also ordered a typewriter, supplies, a cot, and bedding. He walked around the corridors, familiarizing himself with the rest of the labyrinthine building, then looked for the officer's mess.

Returning that afternoon, he found, rather to his surprise, all the items he had requested in place, the lights were on, and a fan was running.

He sat at the table and rolled officially embossed Luftwaffe stationery into the typewriter. He then created an initial list of mission needs and concerns.

His initial list included selecting personnel, scheduling transportation, and identifying American contacts; researching the Biltmore Estate, including overhead photos, surrounding grounds, and entrances; obtaining a list of visitors and staff; getting information on the painting, size, weight, location at Biltmore, and security if known; identifying gear needed; and composing an operation plan.

He worked late into the night and slept on the cot.

* * *

The following day, after finishing his breakfast at the mess, he was returning to his new office when he spotted a Luftwaffe enlisted man walking past. Gunther stopped in mid-stride. "Conrad?"

"Sir?"

"Um…never mind. Carry on."

"Yes, sir."

The man looked identical to an acquaintance from boarding school, but the last Gunther had heard, Conrad Muller had been in the U-boat service.

He instantly realized how his old friend could help with his mission. He had last visited his old friend when Muller was a Heidelberg University art major.

He hurriedly went to Goring's outer office and asked Reicher to find Lieutenant Conrad Muller of the German Navy's current whereabouts. He returned to his office and typed Muller's name as team member number one. Then, he started studying the U.S. and North Carolina maps Reicher had provided.

That evening, he slept in the officers' quarters Reicher had arranged for him in the Ministry.

While Gunther was studying the maps the following day, Reicher brought in her findings on the Kriegsmarine's Lieutenant Muller. The International Red Cross had reported Muller as a prisoner of war in a small town outside Crossville, Tennessee. Reicher said she checked with the Abwehr, and their Canadian agents found out this was some special agreement between Roosevelt and King.

This news was unwelcome, indeed. He'd thought he had his first team member—one with the background needed to identify an authentic Mona Lisa—one who could help him devise a plan to capture it. But his first move had been blocked. Not a good start, thought Gunther.

He had dinner in the mess before heading for his quarters. He was surprised to again see the Luftwaffe-enlisted man who so closely resembled Lieutenant Muller. This time, he stopped the corporal and asked his name and where he worked.

The corporal said, "Walter Hellwig, sir. I work in the supply section."

Gunther studied the man closely. He did look just like Muller. He dismissed him and continued to his quarters.

As he lay in his bunk that evening, the outline of a plan began forming.

Perhaps he could free Muller from the camp. To avoid alerting the U.S. that an operation was happening, he wanted to swap his Muller look-alike for the genuine

Muller. He fell asleep, wondering how to reach Tennessee once he got there. Tennessee seemed terribly far inland. He slept very little that night and skipped breakfast to get to his office.

* * *

In his plan, he, Muller, and another team member, maybe from the Abwehr or at least a fluent English speaker, would leave Tennessee and travel to North Carolina. They would switch Goring's copy of the *Mona Lisa*, which Gunther thought of as *Mona Lisa* #2, for the real *Mona Lisa*, which he thought of as *Mona Lisa* #1. They could escape without the Americans even knowing there'd been a theft. They could either head south to Mexico or else make their way to meet a U-boat off the coast and return to Germany. But all this would only work if they were never detected at the POW camp or at the Biltmore.

"But could it really happen," he muttered. He needed to fill in much more detail. He began creating a new, comprehensive list of requirements. They needed at least one more person. Gunther's office had no phone, so he went back to Goring's office and asked Reicher for help accessing records of English-speaking personnel working in the Air Ministry. He also requested that Corporal Walter Hellwig be assigned under his command.

When Reicher delivered service jackets for all English-speaking personnel in the Air Ministry, and Hellwig had reported to him, he explained to the corporal in general terms what they'd be doing. He wanted to run his high-level plan by Goring before he fully briefed anyone.

A perplexed Hellwig, trying to understand what Gunther's vague plan meant for him, said, "This means

I'd be leaving Berlin and not coming back for months or years?"

"Yes, it does, Corporal. Did you not think the Luftwaffe could send you anywhere at any time?"

"I did, sir. But my father is in the Army, and I'm the only one to care for my sick mother. I go home to her every evening. She has no one else."

Gunther wanted to say the needs of the Fatherland came before all else, but instead, he said, "I'll talk to Reicher. I'm sure she can help. For now, sort these service jackets into two groups: those above the rank of Captain and those in the rank of Captain and below. We'll continue our discussion after I talk to Reicher. You will be going with us. You are a key point in my plan."

"Yes, sir. If my mother is taken care of, I'm in. Do you mind if I smoke, sir?"

"That's fine. You need to find a couple of ashtrays."

When sorting was finished, Hellwig handed Gunther the two stacks of service jackets for a final review. Six were above the rank of Captain, and seven were below that rank.

A half-hour later, they had winnowed the jackets down to two. The first was Captain Bruno Schultz. Schultz had studied world history and accounting at the University of California in Los Angeles from 1929 through 1931.

The second jacket belonged to Lieutenant Werner Krauss. Krauss had attended the University of North Carolina at Chapel Hill, receiving a degree in architecture. His record noted that Krauss spoke impeccable American English. Krauss was currently serving in the airfield planning section here at the ministry.

* * *

Captain Bruno Schultz worked on General Hoffman's staff. Gunther decided he should request the captain come to an interview on the Reichmarschall's behalf.

He found Schultz in a small office outside Hoffman's.

"Captain Schultz?"

"Yes, Lieutenant?"

It's going to be one of those situations. He's a captain, and I'm a lieutenant, thought Gunther. "Captain, I'm Lieutenant Rolf Gunther. I work on special projects directly for the Reichsmarschall. I understand you attended university in America."

"The Reichsmarschall and special projects. That's interesting. I attended university in Los Angeles, California, ten years ago."

"I'd like to talk about your time in the States. I'm in room 323. Could you spare an hour?"

"I'm swamped, Lieutenant. I work for General Hoffman, you know."

"I do, captain. And who does the General work for?"

"Point taken, Lieutenant. I'll make an availability in half an hour."

"Thank you, Captain."

* * *

Captain Schultz entered without knocking. Gunther stood. "Time for a break, Corporal."

"Yes, sir," said Hellwig.

"Please have a seat, Captain. The Reichsmarschall is interested in Luftwaffe personnel who speak English and have been to America. Can we carry out this interview in English?"

"As you wish, Lieutenant."

"When were you there?"

"From 1929 through 1931. I attended UCLA in Los Angeles. I studied world history and accounting."
"Did you do any traveling around the States?"
"I did take one weekend to travel south. I visited San Diego, a city with a large naval base, and crossed the border into Tijuana, Mexico. Other than that, I stayed in the Los Angeles area."
"I see. I'm interested in someone who has also visited the Southeastern U.S."
"I never visited there. Aren't they mostly uncivilized and inferior in that area?"
"I don't believe that to be the case. I am aware many Europeans think so."
"What do you know about art, Captain?"
"Don't care much for it, Lieutenant. As der Fuhrer believes, most art nowadays is degenerate."
"Well, thank you for your time, sir. I'll inform the Reichsmarschall you were helpful."
"You're welcome, Lieutenant."
I don't believe the captain will work, thought Gunther.

When Hellwig returned, Gunther asked him to find Lieutenant Krauss and requested he visit Room 323 at his first convenience on a matter of great importance to the Reichsmarschall.

* * *

Krauss tapped at his door an hour later.
"Enter."
He stood ramrod straight, tall at 1.83 meters. Gunther guessed him to be 88 kilos, with light brown hair and green, intelligent eyes. He had the build of an Olympic lightweight wrestler.

"I'm Lieutenant Rolf Gunther; I work directly for the Reichsmarschall. Please have a seat. Would you like a cigarette?"

Krauss declined.

Corporal Hellwig brought coffee from a service set in the corner. He then took a seat out of the way.

"I've visited America multiple times. I'd like to talk to you about the time you spent there. What years were you there?"

"I was at Chapel Hill from 1934 through 1936. I received a degree in architecture."

"Why American architecture? Why not a German university?"

"I'm a fan of Richard Morris Hunt and the classic eloquence style of architecture. My pre-war plan was to open an architecture firm that would serve all of Western Europe, so American architecture was what I wanted to study."

"Where is Chapel Hill?"

"Just outside Durham, North Carolina. In the mountains, not unlike Bavaria, really."

"Do you know how far that is from, say, Asheville?"

"If I remember correctly, it's a little over three hundred twenty kilometers. I had contemplated going to Asheville at one time. As an architecture student, I wanted to visit the Biltmore House near there because its design fascinated me. I never actually got to do that."

"That's interesting. What do you know about the Biltmore Estate? Please answer in English."

"Quite a bit. I took a class on Hunt's great achievement. Hunt was the first American to be admitted to the school of architecture at the Ecole des Beaux-Arts. But, back to the Biltmore Estate, I know it encompasses over ten thousand acres, and the house has two hundred and fifty rooms. The initial building started in 1885, and work on the outer buildings continued into the early 1900s. It's quite an architectural feat. Up to forty staff members once assisted in the estate's operations. The final project of that class was for each student to replicate the building schematics and floor plans. The university library had Hunt's originals."

Rolf could not believe this coincidence, "Do you still have those drawings?"

"I believe they are at my mother's in Dresden. You mentioned special projects. May I ask what kind of special projects? Do you mean...rockets? Or, special new planes?"

"We'll get to that in a moment. Would you agree to help me create a plan to free a prisoner of war from a Tennessee camp, execute a theft at the Biltmore, and return to Germany?"

Krauss slumped back in his seat, looking stunned. "Wow. That's certainly ambitious. It's not what I saw myself doing in the Luftwaffe. I'll need to think about this for a bit. I'd need to get clearance from my current duties. How would we even get to America? The Royal Navy is still in control of most of the Atlantic."

"The Reichsmarschall will reassign you the minute I ask him. I can give you until tomorrow morning. If you accept, I'd like to introduce you to Reichsmarschall Goring and lay out the high-level plan. If he agrees, you and I will do the detailed planning and develop a timeline and material requirements. Currently, the team would be made up of you, Corporal Hellwig, and myself. I haven't yet decided on how we'll get there or a lot of the other specific details; among other items, we'll need contacts and transportation in America. I'll see you back here first thing in the morning for you to give me your answer."

* * *

Gunther was in his office by 0630. Krauss got there at 0715, and Hellwig let himself in a moment later. Gunther introduced Krauss to Hellwig and asked if they had both had breakfast or wanted coffee or tea. Both declined. He lit a cigarette and asked Krauss what he'd decided.

"I still believe this operation is ambitious, but I'll agree to help plan it. I'll feel more confident about volunteering when I can see a plausible op plan, especially to get us there and back."

"Good," said Gunther. "I'll tell the Reichsmarschall we have the nucleus of a team and a high-level plan. I'll contact his secretary to see when he's available. Also, teach Hellwig here a few basic English words every chance you get."

"Yes, sir."

"In the meantime, Corporal, locate a large map of the North Atlantic showing the coast of France and the east coast of the southeastern United States.

"Lieutenant Krauss, contact the Naval Ministry. Find out where we have submarine bases in the captured French territory. If you encounter any difficulty, say this is for an operation of the Reichsmarschall. If you have further difficulty, have them contact me, and I'll go over and show them my orders. If we still encounter problems, I know of someone who is friends with both the Reichsmarschall and der Fuhrer. He could get that information from Admiral Raeder and still keep this project secret.

"Let's all meet back here at 1300. I'll let Reicher know we'll be available after 1300."

Gunther, Krauss, and Hellwig were all back in Gunther's office at 1300 hours. Gunther told them that the General would see them at 1400. Hellwig had rolled in a large map of the North Atlantic.

Krauss walked to the map, looked at his notes, and then said, "From where we have established U-boat bases, the closest point to the U.S. is out of France. We are currently constructing bomb-proof U-boat bunkers in Brest, Saint Nazaire, La Rochelle, and Bordeaux. Construction is eighty percent complete in five operational pens at La Rochelle. All sites are scheduled to be completed by late this year or early next year. La Rochelle appears to be our best option. Kriegsmarine schedules are top secret, and it would take an intervention from the Reichsmarschall to access them or to schedule a U.S. insertion."

"Well done, Krauss."

* * *

Three hours before, Gunther had asked Reicher, using her authority as the Reichsmarschall's secretary, to contact the Abwehr and discuss the logistics of landing personnel in America. Reicher had briefed Gunther a half hour ago. He marked the U-boat bases on his map of the Atlantic. After studying the map, he confidently placed pins on the East Coast of the states of North Carolina and South Carolina. This map version only showed the U.S. halfway through East Tennessee, which would work for now. However, only Knoxville, Nashville, and Chattanooga were named. He couldn't locate Crossville. He remembered his original info on the POW camp, stating it was in East Tennessee. This was the best he could do at the moment. He temporarily stuck a pin midway between the three cities.

At the Reichsmarschall's office, Goring came around his desk to greet them. He was wearing one of his custom-made, non-regulation uniforms. Gunther introduced Krauss and Hellwig.

Goring nodded amicably. "Have a seat, gentlemen." He sat on the other couch. "Gunther, tell me what you've got."

"Thank you for seeing us, General. Here is the plan so far. We take a U-boat to the Carolinas. We make our way to the POW camp in Tennessee with some contact and transportation help in the U.S., perhaps from the Bund, Mr. Lindbergh, or your New York contact. We switch Corporal Hellwig here, almost a twin to Lieutenant Muller, at the POW camp in Tennessee. Muller is an expert on the paintings of da Vinci and can verify we're getting the real thing. Muller, Krauss, and I will go to Asheville and the Biltmore Estate. We'll need an inside contact; I'm working on a plan. After watching the estate to identify security patterns, we'll switch your Chaudron copy with the real one. If all goes well, there will be no alarm or pursuit as we go to the East Coast for extraction via a U-boat."

The Reichsmarschall sat thinking. "Do you have a timeline?"

"I'm working up one, sir. We must estimate the travel time for a U-boat from France. This has the largest impact on our overall plan."

Goring sat stroking his ample chin. "It just might work. Excellent work, Lieutenant. You might need more authority when dealing with Raeder and Doenitz's people at the Kriegsmarine. I'm promoting you to captain, effective immediately. And I'm grateful to Corporal Hellwig here for volunteering to sit out the war in a prisoner-of-war camp. I'm promoting him to sergeant, effective immediately."

Hellwig started to protest, "Sir, I'm not sure…" But Gunther cut him off. "Thank you, sir; Hellwig is an integral part of our plan."

"Great," said Goring. "I'll have Reicher complete the paperwork. Show me the completed operation plan with your timeline and budget when it's ready. Let me know when you need my Mona Lisa." He waved at the wall. "Dismissed. Oh, and Reicher has your new written orders."

Once back in their office, Krauss congratulated the two on their promotions but seemed less than enthusiastic. Was he jealous, Gunther wondered?

Gunther showed the other two his orders, with the letter stating he represented the Reichsmarschall. They got to work roughing out a list of tasks and materials. Gunther also attempted to piece together a budget.

At 1700, Reicher knocked. She handed Gunther a set of promotion orders for himself and Hellwig. She also handed Gunther captain's collar tabs and a pair of sergeant's stripes for Hellwig.

"Thank you, Sergeant! That was thoughtful of you to include the captain's tabs and sergeant's stripes," said Gunther.

Reicher returned to her office. Gunther turned to present the sergeant's stripes to Hellwig.

Hellwig said, "We still haven't addressed my mother's needs, Captain. I'm not going unless we satisfactorily address that."

"It will be taken care of, Hellwig. You're going."

Krauss shook his head.

Gunther returned to the timeline. The U-boat's schedule would dictate the rest of the timeline. They also required the route to East Tennessee from their landing point in the U.S.

THREE

RANDOLPH FIELD, TEXAS
OCTOBER 14, 1941

Freshly promoted to the rank of captain, Donahue fidgeted at the same small desk in the same small motor pool office he'd occupied since his release from the hospital.

He was reading a set of transfer orders. "Crap," he muttered. "Not Carolina." He was too far from Alaina here in San Antonio. *At least here, I've been able to see her on some weekends. North Carolina is much too far.*

The transfer orders directed him to report to the Army's Morris Field in North Carolina. "What the heck!" he muttered. Other than Bragg, he was unaware of any other field in North Carolina. Where in the world was Morris Field even located?

He went to the file cabinet to see if he had a map. He was lucky to find an old Standard Oil gas station map. Morris Field wasn't on it, so he called in the motor pool's master sergeant and asked if he'd ever heard of a Morris Field.

"Sure, I've got a buddy stationed there. It's near Charlotte. Brand new. They transferred him there two months ago. I think a bird colonel runs it."

"Thanks, Sarge. What's your buddy's name?"

"Pay, Neldon Pay, Sergeant First Class."

Donahue's orders read, For Further Transfer. That meant Morris wasn't his final destination. The Commanding officer would brief him once he got there. He could use his privately owned vehicle and be reimbursed for mileage. He was to report at 0800 on October 20, 1941.

Donahue had nothing more to do here but pack up his propeller, puzzle box, and uniforms, check out with the CO, and hit the road. He hoped his heap of a Ford would complete the trip. The arrival date didn't even give him time to drive to Lubbock and personally say goodbye to Alaina.

He called her, and they talked for twenty minutes. She understood military life, but that didn't make it any easier to say goodbye. He told her it was unlikely he would be able to come back for Christmas, but he would write. He asked her to send a photo once he sent her his mailing address.

When he reached East Texas, his drive started to improve. The leaves in Arkansas and Tennessee turned into a beautiful array of Fall colors. The Ford broke down only once in Maryville, Tennessee. After installing a new coil, he was on his way East again.

He arrived a day early, so he spent the day touring Charlotte and even went to a movie theatre, seeing *Never Give a Sucker an Even Break*, starring W.C. Fields.

MORRIS ARMY AIR FIELD
OCTOBER 20, 1941

The following day at 0800, he was sitting outside the commanding officer's office. Colonel Artis Powell greeted him. Though Powell was a relatively small man, his service ribbons included a Distinguished Flying Cross and a Purple Heart. He'd seen action. *But where,* Donahue wondered? The U.S. wasn't at war—not yet, anyway. *Maybe some of our actions in Central America.*

"Let's go into my office," said Powell. "Your orders are some of the strangest I've seen. They want you at Biltmore House outside Asheville. You'll introduce yourself there to Mrs. Cornelia Vanderbilt Cecil and her husband, John. They're expecting you. You will also meet Daniel Roberts from the National Gallery and two French curators. There'll be a U.S. Army master sergeant, and fourteen enlisted who'll act as security detail under your command. I gather you're to guard National Gallery works of art. How you arrange the troops, Mr. Roberts, the Frenchmen, and the Biltmore staff is up to you. Once your detachment is in place, you'll relieve the North Carolina highway patrolmen currently securing the grounds."

He looked over rimless glasses. "This is a rather strange set of orders, wouldn't you agree? I'm not sure what help I can supply from my command. Jeeps? Small arms? C-rations? Any thoughts or questions?"

"The Biltmore. Sheese. I'm afraid I don't even know where to begin," said Donahue. "I may take you up on the jeep. Let me see what the detachment brings with them. Do I mostly report to this Roberts? When am I expected?"

"You're due the day after tomorrow," said Powell. "If I were you, I'd consider him your point of contact until we hear otherwise. He's the only U.S. official on site. I believe he'll mostly defer to you."

Donahue got to his feet. "Sir, let me go back to my quarters and digest all this. I'll return tomorrow, if you're available, and ask any questions I might come up with and to check out with you. Do you have any idea who picked this security team?"

"These orders came from Washington. It feels like it might have had some political input."

"Roger, Colonel." He saluted.

Returning the salute, Powell said, "Good luck, Captain."

Back in his room, Donahue drafted a list of tasks he felt he should start with once he arrived at the Biltmore. He'd ask the Highway Patrol what they were doing, review the location of the artworks, and see what internal security was being implemented.

* * *

The next day, he checked out with Powell and motored toward Asheville. The drive took him the rest of the day, and he spent the night at a tourist cabin.

Early the next morning, he drove up to the Biltmore House. The estate was beautiful, but the House itself was grander than any Donahue had ever seen in America, and he'd been to Newport, Rhode Island. He'd seen the estates on the famed cliff walk, but this grand dame surpassed those mansions.

As his tires crunched on the long shell entrance drive, a highway patrolman stepped from the covered foul-weather entranceway and held up a hand. Donahue showed his ID and his orders. The patrolman led him to a side entrance, where they found a staff butler. The patrolman told the butler who Donahue was and turned Donahue over to him.

The butler introduced himself as Randolph. He took Donahue to a grand library. He told him he'd locate the Cecils and tell them he was waiting.

As he waited, he looked around the dark wood library at the thousands of books lining three walls. Rolling ladders were on those three walls, eight easy chairs in red fabric, and three large tables and a desk were placed around the room. A large fireplace was centered on the fourth wall, and old-looking paintings decorated the walls around the fireplace. A bust, which Donahue guessed was of George Vanderbilt, sat on one of the tables. Looking up, he saw a large, beautiful ceiling painting of angels and chariots. I wish Alaina could see this, he thought.

Cornelia Cecil and her husband, John, entered together. Mrs. Cecil was not as regal-looking as Donahue had expected. She was finely dressed, slim, rather plain, and fragile-looking. John Cecil, though, had an aristocratic look. Old money, perfect teeth, custom-made clothing, and polite but smug mannerisms.

Mrs. Cecil said, "It's a pleasure to meet you, Captain. We've been expecting you and want to extend any help we can offer." John Cecil smiled and glanced at Donahue's artificial left hand but said not a word.

"Thank you, um, Mrs. Cecil. I'd like to talk to Mr. Roberts and all the staff and meet the French, who I'm told are here. I would like to see where the artworks are located. At some point, I'll check to note all the entry points. I have an Army security team arriving tomorrow, and they'll replace your state police."

"Certainly," said Mrs. Cecil. "We'll have a bedroom set aside for you. If it doesn't work, we'll find a more suitable room. Just let Randolph, our head butler, know."

"Thank you. I'll try to make our arrangements as unintrusive to the family as possible under the circumstances," said Donahue.

"This way, Captain," said Randolph, who'd been hovering in the background. He took Donahue to see his bedroom. Donahue dropped his flight bag there. They proceeded to find Daniel Roberts and the others.

Randolph left Donahue with Roberts, the assistant French curator, and a French policeman.

Donahue said, "I'm Captain Declan Donahue. I've been stationed here as head of security. Here's my identification and my orders."

Roberts glanced at the ID card and read the orders. He nodded to the Frenchmen and handed the documents back. "What do you have in mind, Captain? This is Phillipe Jourdan, assistant curator, and that's Maurice Caron of the Paris police."

Donahue shook the hands of both men.

Roberts continued, "Antoine Buchard, the French curator, and Jules Mathieu, another Paris officer, are sleeping. They work the 8 pm to 8 am watch. I'm here each day from 10 am to 4 pm. Since Antoine is the senior French representative, and the French are always at the side of the Mona Lisa, I've designated Antoine to deal with all matters concerning the watch rotation."

"An Army security detail will arrive tomorrow. At that time, the highway patrol will depart. After the security details are settled, I'll post a plan and share it with Mr. Cecil, you, and Mr. Buchard. It was Buchard, wasn't it?"

"Yes. Glad to have you here, Captain."

"Nice to meet the two of you. I'll drop by this evening to meet the other two. Right now, I think I'll take a look at the house."

Donahue glanced at the rest of the rooms on the second floor. He climbed to the third floor and nosed around a bit. Opening doors and testing locks. He also inspected the fourth floor, which was essentially servants' quarters. During this process, he encountered a staff member who identified himself as Mr. Cecil's valet, Mal Hyman.

"My room's on the fourth floor. Let me know if I can be of any assistance, Captain."

Donahue found Randolph and asked him if he could meet the staff in the basement's eating area. Randolph said, "I can't get all thirty members together simultaneously, but I can split them into two groups at different times. Would that work?"

"Yes, that would. I'll have the first group within a half hour."

When they arrived, Donahue introduced himself as the head of the new security team. He asked each of the staff members what their duties were and where their main functions took them in their daily routine. He thought one of the maids was flirting with him. As a group, he asked them to report anything they considered out of the ordinary or suspicious.

He told them the FBI would be running background checks on them but not to worry, as that was routine for any security plan where the government was in charge.

The butler invited him to join them for lunch when they broke up. "Yes, I'd like to eat with the staff," replied Donahue. Lunch consisted of fried chicken, fresh green beans, sliced tomatoes, and homemade sourdough bread. Having trouble holding a knife with his prosthetic hand, Donahue clawed the meat off with his fork. Other than that slight embarrassment, he genuinely enjoyed the meal. If the staff noticed, no one let on. He caught the same maid eyeballing him again. She was a brunette, slim, and not unattractive.

After lunch, Randolph assembled the people Donahue had yet to meet. He went over the same routine he had used with the first group. He noticed Mr. Cecil's valet was in this group. He saw nothing noteworthy about the male staff. For some reason, the female staff proved more difficult to read.

Afterward, he and Randolph went outside for a smoke, "Say, are there any buildings that could serve as a shelter for fifteen guys and maybe a jeep or two?"

"Yes, sir. There are a dozen unused bedrooms above the stables. In the early days of the Biltmore, they separated the male and female servants. We no longer do it that way. The rooms are now used for storage. They'll need emptying and cleaning, but they should work for your needs. All the staff, except for myself and Mrs. Thatcher, the lead cook, live in the main house now. Mrs. Thatcher and I both have small cottages on the Estate grounds. Of course, many of our young men have joined the services. I myself served in the artillery in the Great War. Have hearing loss in one ear to show for that."

Donahue thanked him for his service and went to check out the stables. It looked like it would be acceptable. The rooms even included electrical heaters. He turned the first room's heater on, and it soon burned red hot. He would check the other rooms later.

He walked the grounds after dinner and once again ate with the staff. He looked for entry points and positions in which a sentry might best be placed. He noticed two ventilation grills, which he should check more closely later. He'd think about a roving patrol, should he have enough manpower. Around midnight, he retired to the room the Cecils had provided.

He awoke sometime during the night, sweating, dreaming of his plane crash, and fidgeting with the stump of his arm.

* * *

The following day, he decided his room did not satisfy him. It was too far from the artwork. He would move to another later.

At 0730, a fifteen-man detail, headed by a grizzled master sergeant named Buford Willie Gibbs, arrived in two trucks. The trucks carried the men, their gear, weapons, and Field Rations Type C, or "C-Rats," as the men called them. The trucks also held bedding for the detachment.

Watching from the service entrance, Donahue saw Master Sergeant Gibbs, rangy and fit, have the men unload. As the trucks left, the men fell into formation, and Donahue walked into the courtyard.

Gibbs saluted Donahue as he approached, and Donahue returned the salute. In a matter of seconds, they had sized each other up. Then Donahue viewed his security team. What he saw did not impress him. The master sergeant and a corporal looked experienced, but the rest of the detail appeared to be on their first enlistment. Aside from the master sergeant, whoever had selected his team had clearly not sent him a seasoned detail.

Donahue turned to Gibbs. "Sergeant. Have the men stack arms in the stables and prepare the upper level as billets. I'll find something to serve as the ammo locker. When that's finished, I'll speak to the men. I'd also like to see their personnel records. That will be all for now."

He returned to the main house to find a room closer to the artwork. He again checked out the second and third floors. Unable to visualize the layouts clearly, he found Randolph and asked if there were copies of the floor plans. Randolph felt sure that the library housed a set. He would check. Fifteen minutes later, he returned and took Donahue to the library.

Donahue studied the second—and third-floor layouts. Currently, the National Gallery artworks were stored in the Louis XV Room's corner room, and the eleven sculptures were in the Tyrolean Chimney Room. The curators slept in the Damask Room and the Claude Room, three rooms away from the French cops in the Old English Room. Roberts slept in the Sheraton Room.

Even with a pair of men always with the art, Donahue felt a better setup would be on the third floor, with the art all in one large room and both men within easy view of each other. The new arrangement would also better accommodate Roberts having a regular seat for his daytime shift with the two Frenchmen on watch.

He suggested to Roberts they should store the artworks stacked in their crates, one leaning against the other, in the large third-floor Living Hall. There would even be space for the few statues they'd brought. Roberts would move to the Balcony Room, Mr. Buchard, the lead curator, would relocate to the Hoppner Room, the assistant curator would go to the Walnut Room, the French policemen would share the Watson Room, and Captain Donahue would take the Van Dyke Room. Except for the policemen, each would have his own room.

After inspecting the third floor, Buchard, Roberts, and Donahue discussed this suggestion. Roberts did not see a need for the change, but Buchard felt it was a good suggestion. Roberts finally agreed, and they approved moving the artwork the following day. Satisfied, Donahue lugged his bag to his new room.

Back at the stables, Donahue asked Gibbs for the men's service jackets. "Yes, sir. They're on that camp table. Are you sure you wouldn't like me to go through them for you? I've already glanced through them on the ride over."

Donahue picked up the stack. "I've got them. I'll try to work out some hot meals so the troops won't have to eat C-rats all the time. Fresh milk's cheap here, and fresh eggs might be available. The upper rooms in the stable already have heaters. We'll need to check the fuses to see if they'll take the electrical load. It's been some time since they were used. I've only checked the heater in one room. There'll be plenty of ventilation to set up a small cooking area in the open alcove entrance to the stables, but it will still be pretty cold after sundown. Keep it away from the stacked rifles. I'll see the men now. No need to have them fall in."

The men gathered in a semi-circle in the courtyard. Donahue stood to the side, viewing his two non-comms. They presented a striking contrast. Gibbs was slim and rangy, at least 6' 2", looking like he'd just stepped out of a Western film. Corporal Gatlin, in contrast, was 5" 7", if that, and stocky, with the look of a professional boxer with a perpetual chip on his shoulder. Randolph Scott and Tony Canzoneri, Donahue thought.

Donahue stepped up, introduced himself, and summarized why they were there and what they would be doing. He noticed a few men glancing at his prosthesis, gripping the stack of service records against his left side. Deciding to get that distraction out of the way, he said, "I lost my left arm in a flying accident. The Army allowed me to stay on active duty. I've learned to live with it. Does anyone have questions? Now's the time to speak up."

No one seemed to have anything, so he turned to Gibbs. "Sergeant, draw up a security plan. In the meantime, post sentries at the corners of the main house. Relieve the guard every four hours and give me a schedule for the next week. That'll be all."

"Yes, sir!" Gibbs saluted.

Donahue walked to the main house, where he told Randolph what guard positions they had posted. He requested Randolph run it by the Cecils.

"Is it okay if I eat most of my meals with the staff?"

"Certainly, Captain, but I'm sure the Cecils will invite you to eat with them occasionally."

I'd rather not, thought Donahue.

After dinner, he moved his few extra clothes and his propeller to the third floor. Leafing through the service jackets, he discovered that Master Sergeant Gibbs had retired from the Army but had been recalled to active duty just the month before. He also noted that Corporal Gatlin had been a sergeant two months ago. One evening, he had returned to his base while drunk and was confronted by his lieutenant, whom he'd slugged. Also, in Donahue's notes, a Private First Class Ballard had completed a year of college before joining the Army. None of the other men stood out.

Tomorrow, he would search for suitable office space close to his men for himself and his top noncommissioned officer and set up Ballard as the squad clerk.

* * *

The following day, after grabbing toast and coffee, Donahue found Gibbs at the stable area, drinking a canteen cup of coffee. "I'm going to find us an office, Sergeant. Did the guys bunk down okay?"

"They did, sir. Only two rooms had non-working heaters. We're working on that. The carpenter shop is at the other end of the stables if we need any repairs. We can either get assistance or borrow some tools."

"Very well. How did the eating arrangements work?"

"I set up a detail in the entrance of the stables. It's not the best, but we won't starve."

"As I said, I'll see if I can't get some hot food from the kitchen occasionally sent out. I'll let you know each time before it is scheduled to come out so you don't start preparing your C-Rats for that meal."

"That should keep the morale up. You thought about any time off, sir?"

"Good thinking, Sarge. I'll come up with a plan. One last thing," said Donahue. "I noticed the Cecils still have four or five horses at the far end of the stables. Did, um… any stable noises interrupt the men's sleeping?"

"No, sir. I don't believe so. These stables are huge. Personally, I enjoy horses. I was never a Horse Soldier, but I enjoyed riding. Did a lot in my teen years. I'll keep an eye on them, sir. It's colder than usual in this area. We don't have the field jackets and other cold-weather gear we'll need for our sentries. I'm concerned about that."

"I'll phone in an order to Morris Field Supply. In the interim, I'll find an Asheville store that sells camping gear. That'll at least get us heavy socks, gloves, and watch caps."

"Yes, sir. I'm sure the men will be thankful for those."

He needed an office, but he didn't want one in the stables or the carriage house. Heading back to the kitchen, he asked where he might find Randolph at this time of day.

"He could be anywhere at this hour, sir. His office is just off the front door entrance," said a cook.

To the right, as one entered the front entrance, he found the head butler in a medium-sized office. "Hello, Randolph. I hope I'm not catching you at a bad time."

"There never seems to be a good time, Captain, but you're not interrupting. How can I assist you?"

"I'll need an office. I'd rather not set up in the stable."

"Yes, sir, of course. Mr. Cecil suggested I offer you mine if you asked for one. I'm not in here much during the day."

"Thanks, but I'd need something closer to my men. I noticed two spaces that looked like temporary storage or a pre-check delivery station. They're opposite each other as you enter the basement level of the kitchen courtyard."

"Yes, sir. The National Gallery people are eating in one of those. You can have the other. Would you like equipment?"

"A small desk, a medium-sized table, a typewriter if you have a spare, and four chairs would do nicely."

"I'll take care of that immediately, Captain."

"One more thing, can you help me with laundry service for my guys?"

"We have a commercial-grade facility just steps from your office, Captain. If your men could bring in their laundry after 4 pm, we can show them how to run our machines."

* * *

Two hours later, Donahue and Gibbs checked on their new space. The furniture had been delivered, and though the desk's legs were crooked, everything else looked fine.

There was a brand-new Remington Noiseless typewriter with two extra ribbons.

"The table will be your desk, Sergeant. When we have typing to do, we'll bring in Ballard. Do you have a watch rotation yet?"

"Yes, sir, but we do not have a security plan yet. I'll get right on that. Should I try to get a coffee pot here?"

"The kitchen is less than twenty-five feet away. There is always fresh coffee there. I think that will do for you and me. You might get a larger coffee pot and supplies for the men in the stables area. And a radio if you can find one. There will not be much to do here when off watch. I noticed someone set up a camp table and a checkerboard already. It was convenient chairs were already being stored in the loft area."

"Yes, sir. Will do."

"I want to speak with the men again."

"Yes, sir. I'll have them in formation at 1600."

"Come and go in our office as you please, Sergeant."

* * *

At 1600, Donahue strode into the stable's courtyard, where the men were mustered in two ranks. He counted twelve. Three were on security duty. He could see one of the sentries standing at the covered foul-weather entrance to the main house, his M1903 slung over his shoulder.

"Afternoon, men. I wanted to give you a little more background on our mission here. We're providing security for some of the United States' most valued artworks from the National Gallery in Washington. I don't know how long we'll be doing this, for months, at least. When I'm given an estimate of how long we'll be here, I'll let you know. I've told Sergeant Gibbs I'll set up occasional hot meals from the main kitchen. Also, I will see if I can work an occasional day off for you so you can go into Asheville or any other reasonable destination within a thirty-mile radius. I'm requesting a jeep from Morris, you can take that, but the first fender bender we get, I'll take that away. I expect you to follow the chain of command if you have any major concerns. Anything minor, go through Corporal Gatlin. If he doesn't resolve it, then Sergeant Gibbs. If it's still unresolved, and I anticipate it will be by then, you can bring it to me. If it reaches me, I better agree it isn't minor. Any questions?"

No one spoke up.

"That will be all."

"Atten-hut! Fall out," said Sergeant Gibbs.

Gibbs followed him into their office. A few supplies were on the corner of the table. Also, Donahue's Chinese puzzle box sat on the corner of his desk. Donahue had moved his twisted propeller to the corner by his desk. Gibbs gave it a puzzled glance but said nothing.

"I've gotten the okay for us to work the laundry room machines. We can use them after 4 p.m. Detail a man to do that. In the morning, I'll introduce you to Randolph, the Head Butler, Mr. Roberts from the National Gallery, and the Frenchmen providing internal security for all the artworks stored on the third floor. We will operate as an outer perimeter. They'll be the inner perimeter. Clear?"

"Yes, sir."

"I'm going into Asheville to get the items we discussed this morning."

"I'll hold the fort, sir," said Gibbs, saluting.

Donahue grinned and returned the salute.

* * *

In Asheville, he soon found a hardware store that sold camping gear. He purchased ten black wool watch caps, thirteen pairs of dark-colored heavy cotton gloves, and fifteen pairs of heavy woolen socks. That was all the store had. The owner said he'd order more socks and more watch caps and deliver them.

Donahue paid for the items, and a clerk loaded them into his car. Donahue stuffed the receipt in his glovebox for the Army to reimburse him.

* * *

On the way out of town, he noted a pizzeria and a restaurant called Dot's All-You-Can-Eat. He thought he'd occasionally order pizza for the troops. Along with that thought, he should have Gibbs set up another table in the stable. Aside from morning calisthenics, the men would need something to do while not on watch. Cards and board games would do for a start. Otherwise, they'd start drifting around the property, horseplaying in the courtyard, or worse yet, begin annoying the female staff.

FOUR

BERLIN
OCTOBER 24, 1941

Freshly minted Captain Rolf Gunther informed Reicher that he needed to speak to Reichsmarschall Goring regarding the resources needed for his special mission.

A half-hour later, Sergeant Reicher tapped at his door. When Gunther opened the door, she said, "The Reichsmarschall will be available at 1600, Captain."

* * *

At 1600, he was in the foyer outside the Reichsmarschall's office. While waiting, he told Reicher, "You've been a big help in fast-tracking this mission."

Standing and stepping around her desk, she motioned him into Goring's inner office, "Thank you, Captain. I am here should you need anything at all."

Gunther found the portly Marschall already occupying one of the two massive couches, sipping brandy from a ruby red and gold trimmed snifter. He was now wearing an all-white custom-made uniform. He motioned for Gunther to join him. As he sat, Gunther noticed the *Mona Lisa* copy was missing from its prominent position on the wall. In its place was a remarkable painting Gunther did not recognize. The subject was a man with a cane standing on top of a mountain.

"Progress?" said Goring, lifting and draining the snifter.

"Sir. I have several items I need before we can finalize our plan. Reicher has been especially helpful in fulfilling all my requests, but I'm afraid she can't help with these. They will take your assistance to get what we need from our agents in America and from the Kriegsmarine."

Goring nodded as if he knew he'd eventually have to use his position. "And, what would those be?"

"First, sir. I apologize for bringing such small details to you; however, you told me you wanted to remain involved. If you prefer, I'll work through your adjutant, Major Klein, or General Weiss."

Looking distracted, Goring poured himself another brandy. "For now, keep me involved."

"Yes, sir. I'll leave this list for Reicher with you then. It includes United States identification for Seth A. Brown as myself, Jonathon K. Turner as Lt. Krauss, and Christopher F. Wagg as Sergeant Hellwig. If we can access Lieutenant Muller's Navy records, I'd like his ID to be Charles J. Johnson. We'll need winter clothing made in the U.S., including in Muller's size, two U.S.-made flashlights with red lens covers, and extra batteries. We'll need 3-shelter halves like the U.S. Army uses. Any camping store in the U.S. sells them. We'll need three American Boy Scout backpacks and three Scout canteens. We'll also need currency and roadmaps for the Southeastern states. I'd also like two Scout folding knives, high-quality bird-watching binoculars, and a Southeastern U.S. bird-watching book."

"What's your cover story?"

"We'll be graduate students at the University of North Carolina at Chapel Hill. Krauss once studied there and will take the lead on our cover.

"Concerning other needs, sir. We'll need your American contact to have transportation available at Yaupon Beach, North Carolina, starting mid-November. In addition, we'd need a list of staff members at Biltmore House and all visiting guests. Perhaps the source who initially told you about the artwork could get that for us. I believe that is the only access we have at the moment. I hope to get a second source if I can find any possibilities on the staff list. This will be a critical piece of the plan. Can you tell me the position of the person who gave you the tip about the painting?"

"It is my understanding she's a maid."

"I see. If I can't find someone inside with a higher standing than that, entering the house will be much more difficult. I doubt a maid can get or control much about Biltmore's current security measures.

"One last thing, sir. We'll need a priority flight from Berlin to La Rochelle. If you can use your influence with Admiral Doenitz, we will need a fast submarine and a skilled captain to take us from La Rochelle to the Carolinas. I can give you firmer dates when I have the requested items.

"We have our look-a-like to exchange for Muller. We know where we're leaving from and landing in the United States. We'll have to make our Tennessee plan after we have surveilled where Muller works off-base from the POW camp. We have floor plans of the Biltmore House. I'm reviewing these. I can't add more until I know the transportation details and the security at the target."

"Very well, I'll have Reicher send to New York first thing in the morning. Let me know if you need anything else."

"Thank you, General. I'm not at a place where I can tell myself, 'This just might work,' but I believe I'll get to that point if we can get these items."

"You're moving fast, Rolf. Let's not overlook anything. Aside from the Kriegsmarine, do we need to bring in other departments?"

"Since you can control our flight requests, I can't think of a reason for other departments at this time, sir. Reicher has worked some with the Abwehr already."

"Do you have time to have dinner with me this evening, Rolf?"

"Yes, sir. I'm waiting on the items I've just requested, and I'd like to give Krauss and Hellwig a night off."

"Meet me in two hours in the General Officer's Mess."

"Thank you for the invite, sir. I'll see you at 1900."

JAGEMANN GALLERY
NEW YORK CITY
OCTOBER 27, 1941

Although still early, it was a hot day for late in October. More pedestrians were on the street outside the Gallery than were usually out in late Fall.

Lillian was surprised when a messenger service dropped off a package at midday.

Opening it, she pulled out two flimsy teletype sheets from the German Consulate. Five thousand dollars in hundred-dollar bills were also included.

A cover letter contained instructions. Reichsmarschall Hermann Goring would like her help obtaining the items on the enclosed list. He needed Lillian to contact her sister and get a list of everyone staying at Biltmore. He needed these items urgently, and the cash was hers to use for expenses as required.

Goring's list included a vehicle for Yaupon Beach, North Carolina, available by mid-November; a list of everyone working or staying at Biltmore House; any information about what National Gallery artworks were at Biltmore; and any information about security around it.

* * *

Lillian dropped the list on her desk, pulled out her cigarette holder, and lit up a Lucky Strike. She propped her chin in her hands and mentally listed the pros and cons of addressing Goring's request. Her first thought was that if she didn't report this contact at once, she would be a traitor to the United States and, if caught, likely a prisoner for the rest of her life.

But her greed overrode any punitive concerns she might have. Also, the five thousand in cash offered the opportunity for more down the road. She badly needed money.

Faster than she should have, she decided she would comply with Goring's request. She would try to gather his information and ask for more money to arrange things once she forwarded his information. Apparently, whatever he had in mind wouldn't work without her assistance, and Lillian would milk that. Maybe back in Germany?

She started her own list. *How could I get transportation waiting in Yaupon Beach, North Carolina,* wondered Lillian. *Where in hell was that, anyway?*

She needed a map. Finishing her cigarette, she placed her freshly started checklist and her cigarette holder in her drawer. She emptied the ashtray on her desk and told her assistant she'd be taking an early lunch.

She'd thought it was late in the year for tourists, but they clogged the sidewalks. The panhandlers, too, were out in force. Even though the Depression was still on in New York, you could easily forget war was flaring across the Atlantic.

Entering Biblo & Tannen's bookstore on Fourth Avenue, she found a map. Next to the maps was a selection of world globes. She picked one up. *Since I'm going to be traveling. I could use one of these to help me plan my new life.*

She paid for her purchases and stopped at a nearby deli, where she ordered a corned beef sandwich and returned to her gallery.

She told her assistant she didn't want to be disturbed and shut her door. While pulling out her checklist, she started munching on her sandwich.

Checklist item number one: Transportation. She opened her map and found Yaupon Beach, North Carolina.

She mused aloud, "I could pay cash for a car and drive it to North Carolina. But how would I get back to New York?" Looking at her map, she might fly into Columbia, South Carolina, buy a used car under an assumed name, and then drive to Yaupon Beach. She could then take a taxi to the nearest airport and fly home.

Where would I leave it?

Other options? Do I even know anyone in North Carolina? She'd once visited her sister in Asheville, but that had been on an art-buying trip with Martha Gooden, one of her repeat customers at the gallery. It had been a one-day stopover thing. Martha had relatives on the Coast near Myrtle Beach. Martha and her husband Matt had purchased a bungalow on Pawley's Island and owned an older Ford sedan, which they left parked there year-round. Martha had even offered to let Lillian stay for free if she ever got to South Carolina. She'd jokingly told Lillian an extra key was under a flowerpot on the front porch and, chuckling, had said, "Unless a hurricane blew it away."

Lillian couldn't remember any other details, she had jotted the information down on the notes from that buying trip with Martha. If the Goodens still had that property, that might answer her needs. She doubted they would be there in November, but she could send a telegram to check that out.

Checklist item number two: The names of the staff at Biltmore. This was harder. She could ask Elise, but her sister was not a German sympathizer. Elise had been only five when they immigrated. She didn't have the fond memories Lillian had. Getting her help would entail something else—maybe money. Elise was unmarried and made very little as a maid. *I could offer her twenty-five hundred dollars. I hope I'll be getting more from Germany.*

Picking up the phone, she asked for a long-distance operator and called the Biltmore House. Randolph answered. Lillian told him her husband was very sick and she needed to talk to Elise.

After Elise answered, Lillian said, "If the butler asks, I'm telling you Stanley is very sick. He's not, but I was hoping you could call me for a private chat when you can get to another phone. It's important and urgent, Elise."

"Oh my, Oh my. Can you at least hint at what it's about?"

"I've come into some money, and I'd like to share it."

"Oh! I'm off tomorrow. I'll call you tomorrow from a pay phone in Asheville."

"Thank you, *mein schwester*. *Ich liebe dich*. We'll talk tomorrow."

DALEWOOD DRUG STORE
ASHEVILLE, NORTH CAROLINA
OCTOBER 28, 1941

Elise placed a collect call to New York City.

"Jagemann Gallery."

"It's me."

"Wonderful! Good morning, sister. Here's why I called in such a hurry. I have new clients who've offered me a substantial fee for information about which artworks are stored at Biltmore. They'd also like a list of everyone staying there. We'd get more if I could give them specifics on the guard setup. A lot more."

Elise gasped, not believing what she'd just been asked to do. She whispered, "They're planning to steal them!"

"Listen to me, dear sister. It's no loss to the National Gallery. All these paintings are overinsured. They'll only miss a few when they bring them back, and they have hundreds to display. This is no loss to the public. And you and I will be well off for the rest of our lives."

Lillian did not mention the *Mona Lisa*.

Elise furtively looked around the store. Was that old man eavesdropping? She cupped the phone and lowered her voice. A little less shocked, she said, "I don't know, Lillian."

Lillian, moving in to close the deal, said, "Didn't you once tell me you'd love to move to California and work for one of the movie stars? You would have the means to do that and more with what we're being offered. I even see some follow-up money in this."

Elise was silent for a moment. "How would it work?"

Lillian knew Elise had come around. "My clients gave me some up-front money. I could wire twenty-five hundred dollars. You should have your bank call my bank for the specifics. Do you have a pencil?"

Elise hesitantly opened her purse. She tore a small corner from the phone book. She hesitated, then said, "I'm ready."

Lillian opened her drawer and pulled out her last statement. "Have your bank call New York City. The number is Madison 4297. Then, ask for Mr. Belmont. When he comes on the phone, hand the phone to your bank officer. That's all. They will complete the transfer. You'll have it in your account by tomorrow or the next day."

With a sigh, Elise said, "Tell me again what you need?"

Lillian reiterated her list. "Any painting titles you can provide. Importantly, a list of everyone staying at Biltmore. We'll get extra if we can give them specifics on the security. I need it as soon as possible, Elise."

"I'll do what I can do. I'll go to my bank now and get them to call."

"Thank you, dear sister," said Lillian. "This time next year, you'll be on a casting couch with Errol Flynn."

BILTMORE HOUSE
OCTOBER 30, 1941

Elise went to her bank and followed instructions. The bank officer said the money would be in her account in two or three days.

She started her new side job as she went about her regular cleaning routine. All the prior evening and night, she'd thought about what Lillian wanted. Aside from the one painting she'd heard the Frenchmen talk about, she knew little about what was stored here. Heck, she knew nothing about the paintings regularly on the walls here but that they needed to be dusted weekly. Thinking about it now, she felt sure some of those were valuable. Would they do a holdup and rob the staff, too? She was already sorry she'd agreed.

She had better luck getting the names of people here. A desk drawer in the kitchen held the complete list of anyone needing meals. The head cook checked the list every morning, and Randolph kept it updated.

She already knew the highway patrol, four Frenchmen, and an American curator handled the security. She spent the rest of the day thinking about how she could get information on the paintings.

Since the county sheriff had interviewed them and completed some sort of background check on all the staff, Elise was now free to return to duties on the house's third floor.

The next day, she deviated from her routine and entered the third-floor Living Hall, pushing aside the heavy curtain that covered the open doorway. She passed Mr. Roberts as he exited. Two Frenchmen sat guarding the paintings. She waved her feather duster. "Hello there!"

Startled, one of the Frenchmen stuttered, "Ello."

"Would it hurt if I kept these crates dusted once a week?"

The assistant curator looked at the bald-headed policeman, who shrugged and winked at Elise. "I don't think that would hurt anything," replied the first Frenchman.

Elise began dusting, and the first Frenchman went back to reading while the second one checked out her ankles.

As she dusted, she glanced around. A manifest lay on a table by one of the heavy curtains that covered the four entryways into the Hall. The curators must have used it as a checklist to ensure no crates were lost in the move. She worked her way around to the manifest. She slowly dusted the desk while trying to memorize the list. Many of the names appeared foreign, and there was nothing simple about them. She struggled to remember at least two titles. Smiling at Frenchman number two and waving her duster as a goodbye, she quickly went to her room to write down the titles she'd memorized. *A Polish Nobleman* and *The Annunciation*. She had earlier written Lillian about the two Frenchmen mentioning *The Alba Madonna*.

The following day, she made up an excuse to Randolph about needing to go to the pharmacy to get some pills she'd run out of. She assured him she'd be back in two hours if he could have one of the gardeners run her into town. "I'm very sorry for the interruption, sir."

"If your regular duties aren't complete this evening, please keep at it until you're done. I'll have one of the cooks set you a plate."

Once in the Dalewood, she called Lillian collect and gave her all the names she'd copied. She also gave her the names of the paintings and described the five men who accompanied the artworks, as well as the highway patrolmen.

Because it was so interesting, Elise also mentioned that morning's accidental meeting with Mr. Cecil's valet, Mr. Hyman. Elise was cleaning his fourth-floor bedroom, directly above Mr. George Vanderbilt's former room, which no one had slept in since his death. It was maintained as a shrine.

As Elise was dusting the windowsill, she heard a noise behind her and turned to find Mr. Hyman coming out of the wall. A door she did not even know existed! "Mr. Hyman, what...!"

"I'm sorry to startle you, Miss Schneider. I needed a fresh handkerchief. I didn't know you were in here. These stairs were for Mr. Vanderbilt's valet, but Mr. Vanderbilt would use them to go from his room directly to the bowling room. He was an avid bowler. Should Mr. Vanderbilt need his valet, he could get to Mr. Vanderbilt's room in one minute via these stairs. I'd say getting from the fourth floor to the bowling room takes me less than three minutes. They're quite handy."

Lillian sounded fascinated by this story. Elise added, "There are probably other hidden doors and rooms I don't know about."

"Thank you, sister. Call if you think of anything else, and keep thinking about the money."

JAGEMANN GALLERY
NEW YORK CITY
NOVEMBER 1, 1941

Lillian again tasked Darla to take a package to her contact at the Consulate. The package included the Biltmore names and the address of 313 Beach Drive in Pawley's Beach, S.C. The keys would be hidden under the flower pot on the front porch. A car key would be hanging on a hook in the kitchen. The use of the beach house was a bonus. She included the new information about security at the Biltmore and the names of three paintings. They were outside the scope of what they'd asked for, but they might also interest the Reichsmarschall and earn her more if he was in a generous mood.

During her planning, Lillian had decided to sell her flailing gallery, leave her increasingly distant husband, and return to Germany, where she thought she would be much more at home. And where, since Jews were being relocated, an Aryan art dealer might find herself sought after. Great possibilities.

The Consulate's office bought the knives, shelter halves, binoculars, a bird watchers journal, and a book on North American birds. They also included winter clothing for four men.

The Consulate packed and forwarded all this information and the requested items. The package departed with the next diplomatic pouch. Once in Germany, they would quickly be sent to the Reichsmarschall's office.

* * *

Sitting in their Chevrolet on the street outside 1435 Massachusetts Avenue, FBI Special Agents Mitch Massingale and Luther Emerson were four hours into their daily surveillance detail.

Luther was admiring a beautiful woman approaching the iron gates of the Consulate. Suddenly, he sat straighter in the passenger seat. "The Betty Grable look-alike. She was here last month."

Darla entered the compound and exited again five minutes later.

"We need to speak to her," said Mitch.

The agents started their car, made a U-turn, and cruised behind Darla for two blocks. Seeing an open space ahead, they pulled to the curb, and Luther stepped out. "I'm sorry to bother you, miss, but I'm with the Federal Bureau of Investigation." He showed Darla his badge. "Are you an employee of the German Consulate?"

"No, I'm not," said Darla.

"Would you mind coming down to headquarters to answer a few questions? "

"I'm not sure. What's this about?"

"We're interested in what you saw in the consulate," said Mitch from inside the car.

"Will this take long? I have to get back to work."

"It should not," said Luther. He opened the rear door.

Mitch and Luther took Darla to the fourth-floor interrogation room. Once Darla was seated, Mitch offered her water or coffee. She declined both.

"What is your name, Miss?"

"Darla Patton."

"Are you a German citizen, Miss Patton?"

"No, I'm not," said Darla, glancing around the small room.

"Do you mind telling us what you were doing inside the Consulate?"

"My boss asked me to deliver a package."

"Is your boss a German citizen?"

"I don't know. I believe she came here as a child."

"Do you know what was in the package?"

"No, of course not."

"What is your boss's name?"

"Lillian Jagemann. She and her husband own the Jagemann Gallery."

"So, you were running an errand for your employer?"

"That's correct."

"Is this the first time you've done this?"

"No. The second."

Mitch glanced at Luther as if asking, you got anything else? Luther shook his head.

"All right, Miss Patton. I believe that is all we need. We'll take you back to your workplace. I believe we should talk to Mrs. Jagemann."

The agents drove Darla to the Jagemann Gallery.

Going in with them, Darla saw Lillian and tried to tell her what had happened. The FBI agents cut her off. "Are you Mrs. Jagemann?"

"I am," said Lillian. "Who are you? Is there a problem?"

The agents identified themselves and showed their badges. "Can we talk in your office?" said Massingale.

"This way," said a composed Lillian.

After closing the door, Lillian offered them seats.

Massingale said, "Miss Patton has acknowledged delivering two envelopes to the German Consulate on your behalf."

"Yes. My parents were German."

"Can you tell us what was in the envelopes?"

"Why would you care? We're not at war with Germany."

"True as that may be, the near future may change that. So, the government is, of course, interested in prospectively belligerent countries. We would like to know what your correspondence was about."

"Stated that way, I think I understand," said Lillian, "My father and mother have passed away, but my father's sister, my favorite aunt, is still in Germany. She lives in Bremerhaven. I was hoping the consulate could check to see if she was safe. Whether she was alive or dead. I also included a letter to my aunt."

"I see," said Massingale. "Has the Consulate gotten back to you?"

"Not yet."

"If I may ask, why did you get Miss Patton to deliver the messages? Why not take them yourself?"

"I have a gallery to run, and we've not been doing well. I'm concerned about my aunt, but also about my business."

Massingale looked at his notes, then nodded to Emerson. "Please send any further correspondence through our office. Thank you for your time."

The agents stood and left.

Lillian went to find Darla. She explained what she had told the agents and apologized for the situation. She told Darla she could have the rest of the day off.

Lillian returned to her office and poured herself a drink. The agents would probably watch her for a while, so she chose not to close the shop.

Sitting in their vehicle down the street from Lillian's gallery, Mitch said, "We should watch her for a while. She seemed very under control to me. Either nothing there, or she's really good."

FIVE

BERLIN
NOVEMBER 4, 1941

Reichsmarschall Goring opened the box from America.
    He was especially interested in seeing who was at the Biltmore. And, of course, if any security information was included. He first saw the list of paintings. The *Mona Lisa* was not mentioned. *Interesting. Tighter security, probably. I'd like to own the other paintings listed,* he thought.
    Scanning the roster, he paused at Antoine Buchard's name. Goring had, of course, heard of Buchard. He was considered the world's authority on Leonardo da Vinci's works, primarily the Mona Lisa. The last Goring had heard, Buchard was at the Louvre in Paris.
    Goring also knew a little about Buchard's background. The man was of Italian-French descent, having been born in France near the Italian border. Considering his name, the Italian must have been on his mother's side, thought Goring.
    He decided he would find out where Buchard had been educated.

Germany currently had military detachments in Italy, ostensibly to train its allies' troops but mainly to keep the Italians on point regarding what needed to be done in this war. Goring wondered if Buchard happened to have any family members in Italy or France. If so, a squeeze might offer an opportunity to get his cooperation. That would make the entry and the switch a lot less complicated.

He pressed a button on his intercom. "Sergeant Reicher. Find out all you can about Antoine Buchard, head curator at the Louvre Museum. Where does he have relatives, close friends, and universities attended? Any other personal information on him? Make this a priority."

"Yes, sir. Right away."

* * *

Goring summoned Gunther. He handed over the clothes, books, and other items and said, "There is a name on the Biltmore list that may give us our inside contact. Antoine Buchard. I've started researching for relatives and close acquaintances."

"Excellent news, General. If this works out, we'll have filled in a major need in the mission plan. Anything new you'd like me to do, sir?"

"Go through the list and see if you can find a backup if Buchard has no relatives we can use."

"Yes, sir."

After examining the rest of the consulate items, Gunther was pleased. The American IDs appeared perfect, and the information on an automobile and house address excited him.

"Is there any progress on securing a submarine, sir?"

"Actually, Raeder was being coy. But, yes, a boat will be available in as early as eight days if we can be ready. If not, give me a date I can send to him."

"Thank you, General. I'll update our operation plan. I can fill in the timeline now. We are close."

* * *

Luftwaffe Sergeant Greta Reicher had been Goring's personal pick. She was lovely, intelligent, and highly competent. She'd lost her husband, Karl, two years earlier during the invasion of Poland. He was one of the fourteen thousand dead or missing. Goring had the choice of any person in Germany to act as his secretary. He'd reviewed thirty records before interviewing the top three. Greta had been his choice. He found her more valuable than his actual aide, Major Otto Klein. While, on paper, Reicher reported to Klein, Klein knew she only answered to the General.

Reicher made a note of the Reichsmarschall's order about Buchard and added it to her task list. She would call the Museum of Art and the Arts Commission to see if any members knew Buchard personally.

Reaching Ernst Wolfe on the phone at the Berlin Museum of Art, she began, "My name is Sergeant Greta Reicher; I work for Reichsmarschall Goring. He would like to know if you know Antoine Buchard?"

Wolfe said, "I've been to the Louvre and seen him at a symposium on art restoration. I wouldn't say I know him personally. You might contact Ernst Zimmermann at the Arts Commission. I believe they attended the same university while working on their post-graduate degrees."

"Based on your visits to the Louvre, what sort of man would you say Mr. Buchard is?"

"From my little interaction with him, I would say he is quite competent and highly principled, Sergeant."

"Thank you, Herr Wolfe. I'll contact Mr. Zimmermann."

After several attempts, she reached Zimmermann at the Arts Commission. "Herr Zimmermann, my name is Sergeant Greta Reicher. I work for Reichsmarschall Goring. The Marschall was informed that you might know Monsieur Antoine Buchard."

"Yes, Fraulein. We attended the Royal Academy of Arts in London while earning our postgraduate degrees in Fine Arts. I received my doctorate at the Vienna School."

"Excellent, Herr Doctor Professor. Can you give me any background on Monsieur Buchard? The Reichsmarschall is considering recognizing him for his work at the Louvre."

"Really? That's odd. Is Buchard that friendly to the NSDAP? I'm not sure of what you're looking for, Fraulein?" Now, he sounded suspicious.

"Friends, close family, marriages, likes, and dislikes. The Marschall wants to better understand what the man's accomplished. It's well known the Marschall is a serious patron of the arts."

He sounded reassured, "I see. Well, we did get fairly close during our stay in London. Our apartments were next door to each other.

"Antoine was born in France, near the Italian border. Most of his mother's relatives lived in Italy, near Turin. His wife died of pneumonia fairly young. They had no children as far as I can remember. He was close to his maternal grandfather in Turin. I believe his mother and father are dead. He never remarried. When I met him, he was already an expert on da Vinci's works. He seldom drank. I do remember he once tried pipe smoking, but it was too much of a bother. He quit after a month. That's all I can remember."

"Thank you, Herr Doctor. That's a good start. If I need more, I'll call."

"Certainly, Fraulein. Goodbye."

TEMPELHOF AIRPORT
BERLIN
NOVEMBER 11, 1941

Before boarding the Junkers aircraft, Gunther, Krauss, and Hellwig met with Reichsmarschall Goring and Sergeant Reicher in a private lounge. Gunther was surprised Goring came personally.

"The International Red Cross just gave us an update on Muller. He's volunteering to work offsite three days a week at a place called Tea's Dairy Farm. That may help you plan his switch. Good luck, men," said the General.

"We received the information on Buchard's family, Reichsmarschall," said Gunther. "One more thing is needed for our mission. It'll take up to three weeks to cross in the U-boat. During that time, please reach out to your contacts in America and Italy. Set up a call from Buchard's grandfather to Buchard at the Biltmore House. I've been told he can be reached by a separate kitchen phone. Later, but on the same day as the phone call, please get one of our most competent agents in the States to make some delivery there and come up with a reason to speak to Buchard. Have him instruct Buchard to post a yellow signal in the southwest window of the South Tower Room. Buchard should do this once he's alone protecting the Mona Lisa. That will tell us we can enter, and he will be waiting with the painting. If I don't see a sign by late December, I'll know he didn't agree. I'll adjust to fit the situation."

"Take care of that, Reicher," said Goring, "I'm headed to the Wolf's Lair at the Fuhrer's beckoning. *Auf Wiedersehen*, and bring my Mona Lisa back!"

The three placed their gear behind the seats of a waiting BMW 325, stepped into the cramped vehicle, and were quickly driven to the waiting plane.

BILTMORE
NOVEMBER 12, 1941

It was cloudy and gray that morning, and the weather looked like it might get worse.

At 8 a.m., Buchard was chatting with Jules Mathieu. It was time for them to be relieved from their watch. Jourdan and Caron arrived to take over. Roberts had already arrived early for his duty. On top of one of the crates, he was twirling the coin he often played with.

After leaving the third floor, Antoine decided to get a bite to eat. A cook poked his head inside their eating area. "Mr. Buchard, you have a telephone call."

Puzzled, Antoine walked to the nearby phone nook and picked up "Buchard."

Speaking Italian, a voice said, "Tony, it's me, Luigi. It's Nonno." Antoine wondered how his grandfather, in Italy, would know to call this phone number. He also wondered how a civilian could make a phone call from a war zone.

He'd never received a call at Biltmore before. He had only used the phone once when the *Mona Lisa* had safely reached the House. He'd phoned the head administrator of the Louvre to report that all had gone well and to inquire about how life in Paris was during these uncertain times. To be honest, Antoine had not missed that city since his wife had passed away.

Luigi continued, "Tony, are you there?"

"I'm here, Nonno."

Nonno Giovanni continued, without his usual chitchat, "Tony, they have moved me, Nonna, Sophia, and your aunt, Octavia, to a military compound. We're being treated well, but the officer here insisted I tell you an important contact will visit you soon. He said it would be best if you listened. The officer here said to tell you it greatly affects our well-being. I have to go now. We love you, Tony." The phone went dead.

Antoine hung up. He replayed the call in his mind. He realized what it meant. The Germans wanted the artwork. They would be coming soon, and they were forcing him to help.

* * *

Late that afternoon, a delivery truck from the winery the Cecils used arrived at the service entrance. The driver, in a heavy French accent, asked for the lead cook.

Mrs. Thatcher said, "Yes?"

"I have a special delivery."

"We aren't expecting anything until next week. And it's very late for these things. They are scheduled to arrive in the mornings."

"Yes, ma'am. I apologize for the lateness; my truck broke down north of Asheville. As for this week instead of next, the owners had an exceptional deal on this batch, and they thought the Cecils would appreciate getting their order at half-price."

"Very well. Bring it in and be quick about it!"

"One last thing, madam, I hear a Frenchman from my hometown is staying at the house. A Mr. Buchard? Would it be permissible to say hello? I've not spoken to anyone from my home in over fifteen years."

"That would be highly irregular. Mr. Buchard is a guest."

"Please, madam, I'll not take five minutes of his time, I promise."

"I'll have someone see if he's available. Tell your owners to call ahead the next time they have an unscheduled delivery."

The driver lugged in two cases of cabernet sauvignon. He stood by the service entrance, watching an army sergeant enter a room directly behind him.

After a few minutes, Buchard arrived. "Yes?"

The driver, speaking French, said, "Mr. Buchard, may I speak to you in private, please?"

Antoine, taken aback, stepped into the courtyard. "Who are you, and what do you want?"

In a low voice, the driver said, "I hope the chat with your grandfather was pleasant and informative."

"I asked, who are you?"

"It doesn't matter who I am, monsieur. Listen carefully! It will be of great benefit to your family in Italy. You must be present on an overnight shift where the artworks are stored. Make sure you are alone. When you have arranged it, post a yellow signal in the window of the second or third floor, in the room closest to where you're storing the art; failure to comply will result in your grandparents, and possibly, yourself, suffering a fatal misfortune. Do you understand?"

"You bastards didn't waste any time getting here."

"Neither should you in agreeing. Think long and hard before defying this request." The driver turned away. He started his truck, made a K-turn, and left.

As the driver, a New York station officer in the Abwehr drove off, he mentally noted having observed two sentries, an army sergeant, and an army captain near the stables. There were bound to be more, with a captain in charge, at least company strength; considering the size of the estate, a complete security plan would take a lot of manpower. Currently, they likely had only four sentry posts. He'd noted two and possibly a third on the south terrace while driving out. No roving patrols, although those could be on the other side of the woods. His report would be on its way by coded shortwave that night.

* * *

Antoine stood shaken, then slowly climbed the stairs back to the third floor. What choices did he have here? He knew what they wanted. They likely wouldn't need him if they were not after the world's most famous painting. But how could he betray his country? That would make him another surrendering traitor, like Phillipe Petain, or worse!

He pushed aside the heavy curtain entry to the third-floor Living Hall. He'd brought a cup of tea for Jules. He sat at the table he used for a desk and started doodling on a blank paper. He could think of only two options. The Louvre, as part of the *Mona Lisa's* security plan, always sent their Chaudron copy with the real *Mona Lisa*. He'd always kept it off the manifest. It stayed in his room on all trips; only Phillipe knew of its presence.

So, he had the Louvre's Chaudron copy to work with. Would the thieves have anyone with them who might have the training to detect it as a copy? Would they harm his grandparents if they discovered they'd stolen a fake? Other ugly questions tugged at his mind as well.

BILTMORE
NOVEMBER 14, 1941

On his way to an early breakfast, Donahue met Buchard standing in front of one of the curtains that covered the five open entryways to the Living Hall.

The Frenchman looked stressed. "Good morning, Captain," Buchard said. "Did you sleep well?"

"Morning, Antoine. I did. It looks like you're on the overnight shift; I guess you won't be getting any shut-eye for at least another couple of hours."

"True enough. By the way, I'm glad I ran into you. Two of my compatriots have relatives in the U.S. They would like a week off starting December 19th. Officer Mathieu and I can still cover the shifts while the other two are on holiday. We'll likely go to three eight-hour shifts. Daniel has agreed to take a full shift from 4 pm to midnight. I ran this by him this morning."

"Let me think about it. I'll get back to you," Donahue said.

After an English muffin and coffee, Donahue decided to check on his men's stable arrangements.

* * *

The makeshift barracks included one slightly larger room, which Gibbs was using, and eleven smaller-sized rooms. Two bathrooms on the ground floor each held a sink, tub, and toilet. Corporal Gatlin was next to Gibbs. That left thirteen men for the other ten bedrooms. Gibbs had assigned the most junior privates to share three bedrooms. All the rooms were tight, little more than cells but better than a cold and uncomfortable bedroll on the ground. For there to be no argument over the beds in the three shared rooms, Gibbs had the beds removed, and only bedrolls were used in those rooms. The men did not complain. They had a light, and the heaters worked.

Donahue decided to scout out the rest of the stables and the carriage house to stretch his legs. He found a loft area between the stables and the carriage house. It was large but dusty and empty. If more troops were assigned, they could bunk here. There was no electrical outlet, but they could run extension cords. In the interim, his men could clean it up, add tables and floor lamps, and get a radio. Chairs were stacked in the loft. They could make it their recreation area.

Turning around, he walked back past the bedrooms to the active stables. The four horses looked like they were well cared for. Donahue had seen a groom feed and water them once or twice, but no one seemed to be working with them full-time. While the horses looked well groomed, he'd not seen anyone exercise them. Did the Cecils actually ride? Or were they just for guests?

Past the animals, he found an entry door. He let himself through, not expecting to find anyone, but found a man in a leather apron, running a vintage woodworking planer over a chair back.

The short, husky, Slavic-looking man turned at the creak of the door. He looked to be in his fifties. He wore a wild, Cossack-style gray mustache and a seaman-style black watch cap.

"I'm Captain Donahue, with the U.S. Army detachment here. And, you are?"

"Joseph Ivanovich Konev, head carpenter at Biltmore. As of late, the only carpenter."

"Nice to meet you, Joseph. I'll have my men stay out of your way. In case you haven't noticed, we're billeted at the other end."

"That will be no problem, Captain. If you need my services, I'm glad to help."

"Since you mentioned it, I just set up my office. The desk they gave me is lopsided. When you get a moment? I'm just inside the courtyard, first on the left."

"Why wait? Let's look at it now if you have the time."

Using a double door that opened to the outside, the carpenter led him across the courtyard and into the kitchen courtyard, then through the service doors, turning left into Donahue's office. Gibbs was gone.

Joseph gave the desk a once-over. "It's in sad shape. We could find you another, or I can refinish all four legs. It would be no major task."

"I hate to give you work."

Continuing to evaluate the desk, Joseph eyed the box. "Is this your puzzle box?"

"It is. I was stationed in the Far East in the early 1930s and became fascinated with them. I brought that one home with me. I frequently play with it when trying to think things through." Donahue lifted his prosthetic hand. "It's harder for me to work than it used to be."

Joseph looked at Donahue's hand, then back at the box. "We have these in Europe, also. I believe they originated in Switzerland or maybe England. The boxes were an idea copied from the secret compartments found in nice furniture. I've worked with them. I like them, too. So did Master George Vanderbilt. When I first came here years ago, the shop had a two-foot by two-foot version. The story was that Mr. Vanderbilt noticed them on his travels. He had the two-foot version and a dozen smaller ones shipped here. I tried opening the two-foot version several times but failed. I had much work in those days, so I covered it with canvas. It's still in the corner of my shop."

Donahue thought about Joseph's story. He squinted as a plan began to form. "Joseph, the master cabinet maker! If I opened my Chinese box and broke it down so you could access the pieces, could you make a huge copy? The new box would have to be at least five feet by five."

"That large, Captain? Just curious, why?"

"I need it for something we're here to guard. I can give you the dimensions for the center cavity. Since it's so important to my mission, I can get Mr. Cecil to prioritize it if need be."

"That won't be necessary, Captain. When do you need it?"

Donahue thought about the Frenchmen taking a week off. "I've got about five weeks. I'll bring my box to your shop, and we can open it together."

"All right, Captain. But your desk may have to wait."

"I'll prop something under it. I'll be over within the hour. Can we look at the version Mr. Vanderbilt brought home?"

"Certainly. I'll see you soon, sir." Joseph turned and left.

He went to talk to Buchard but couldn't find him. He was probably still sleeping. Heading to the third-floor Living Hall, he approached the assistant curator.

"Hi, Phillipe, isn't it? Mr. Buchard and I talked about your holiday plans this morning. Tell him I've found something that'll boost security. I'm fine with you taking off for Christmas. Enjoy yourselves."

"Thank you, *mon Capitaine*. I'll gladly inform Antoine," said Phillipe.

* * *

Donahue headed back to his office. Gibbs was in, typing hard and muttering under his breath. "I'll be in the carpenter's shop, sergeant. I want to review your draft security plan before we call it a day."

"Yes, sir, if this friggin' typewriter will cooperate, it'll be ready."

"We said Ballard could do that. Get him in here." Donahue picked up his puzzle box and left.

Back at the carpenter's shop, Joseph had uncovered Mr. Vanderbilt's box and placed it on a workbench. It had alternating yellow, brown, and orange geometric designs on all four sides and a scene of Mt. Fuji with a lake in the foreground on the cover. Tilting it to see the bottom, he admired a large koi fish design.

Donahue sat his box on the same bench and took in the Vanderbilt box. At eight inches, his box seemed miniature compared to the two-foot version.

He felt Joseph looking at him while he looked over the larger box. Joseph said, "Those look like wood inlays, but they are actually fine examples of marquetry and parquetry. Thinly stripped sheets of pictures in wood, that's marquetry; patterns in wood, that's parquetry. The Japanese are masters at this. The thin sheets are applied after the box is built."

"Before we tackle the big one, let me disassemble my box for you to review while I work on the other," said Donahue.

He went through the sixteen sequences it took to open his box. Joseph watched intently. After all the parts were laid out on the desk, Donahue said, "Any questions? Now, let's see if I can open the big one. When I first got hooked on these things, I did a fair amount of research. Looking at the design and the exterior finishings on the larger box, it might be late-19th-century Jap-made. Their wood masters are among the best. Let's see if I can get it open."

Joseph spent some time measuring the pieces of the smaller box, noting the dimensions with a square carpenter's pencil. Donahue began probing the larger one. After thirty minutes, Joseph was through inspecting and measuring Donahue's. "I'll return to some of my work orders, sir. Make yourself at home."

After a half-hour, Donahue had opened only twelve steps. No wonder Joseph gave up after two tries, he thought.

After two more hours of cursing and bruised fingers on his good hand, he'd opened a total of sixteen steps. "I've got to get back to my office. This would have been a great one to copy, but I can't get the damn thing open! This is much cleverer than the tourist box I have. I'll come back tomorrow and try again. We'll use the little box design if you think you can copy that. Perhaps you can incorporate some of these sixteen steps in your design? Watch as I put it back together."

"I can, Captain. I like it. I can even add a number of steps based on what I've seen in European boxes. Also, I have some seasoned exotic wood left over from previous projects. I've got walnut, cherry, rosewood maple, Koa, and curly mango. Not enough to build a five-foot box, but enough to veneer one. That would seem befitting a non-replaceable piece of art. When can you have me the interior measurements?"

"Did I mention storing a piece of art?"

"Everyone working here knows what you're guarding, Captain."

"Of course they do. The storage compartment must be padded and extremely smooth. Or, perhaps, varnished. I'll leave the measurements later this evening or tomorrow." He closed the sequences on Vanderbilt's box.

* * *

Donahue visited the third-floor Living Hall and asked Phillipe to have Buchard look him up before he went on watch that evening.

Back in his office, Gibbs asked if this was an appropriate time to review the draft of the security plan. Donahue said now was fine and pulled a chair up to the table Gibbs used for a desk.

Considering the number of men in the detail, Donahue felt the rotation of the sentries would work out to six four-hour shifts if only three sentries were used. This resulted in some of the men having two watches in a 24-hour period, but this was the only duty they had. The South Sentry post would be covered by one man rotating from the front of the south terrace to the rear every thirty minutes. This should not impact the coverage area since the rear North Sentry had the field of view to the south covered, and the front North Sentry had the field of view to the main gardens at the south end of the house.

Donahue felt Gibbs had done a good job. He made only two changes. "Now, do you feel you've run through all the scenarios and countermeasures?"

"Except for checking the outer perimeter," said Gibbs.

"All right, implement it."

* * *

An hour later, Buchard came in. He didn't look any better than he had early that morning. "You were looking for me, Captain?"

"Yes. You've met Gibbs here?"

"I have. Sergeant."

"Mr. Buchard."

"It's time to get the measurements for the special project I mentioned. The one that'll help protect your, uh, main art piece while your two guys are on leave. Can you give me its measurements? Without the crate, it's currently in?"

"I know those by heart; I can write them down for you now."

"That's great, in inches if you don't mind," said Donahue.

"In American measurement, 23.4 inches by 17.6 inches, including her frame."

"Thanks. I'll let you know if we need a test fitting. Would that be possible?"

"We'll work something out."

* * *

Joseph was in his shop, and Donahue gave him the specs, adding an inch to each dimension just to be sure. "One more request. My two sentry posts at the back of the house are open to the weather. I've gotten the okay from Mr. Cecil for a four-foot by four-foot sentry overhead cover. Could you loan us some tools and materials? One of my guys was a builder before he enlisted."

"Certainly, Captain. Just send him here."

* * *

Donahue stood in the courtyard for a few minutes. He lit a Chesterfield and scratched furtively at the stump under the prosthesis. It itched. Always. And, sometimes at night, the missing arm burned like it was in a deep-fat fryer. *What am I missing? This is going too smoothly. What sort of thief would attempt to steal something from this setup? How would he plan it? What are our vulnerabilities?*

One of the privates looked out, saw him, and ducked back in. He had no field scarf on, and his shirt was misbuttoned. *I'll have to ride herd on these guys. Keep 'em tightened up. Garrison duty, when wars are on their way, the British are being blitzed…we'll be in it pretty soon… but I won't. Damn arm.* He scratched the stump again. Taking one last puff, he flipped the butt into a sand bucket and dropped by the kitchen to get a cup of coffee.

Back in the office, he told Gibbs, "Get Reynolds to see the carpenter for tools and materials to build a shelter for the rear north sentry. Double-check that the other posts have somewhere to step out of bad weather."

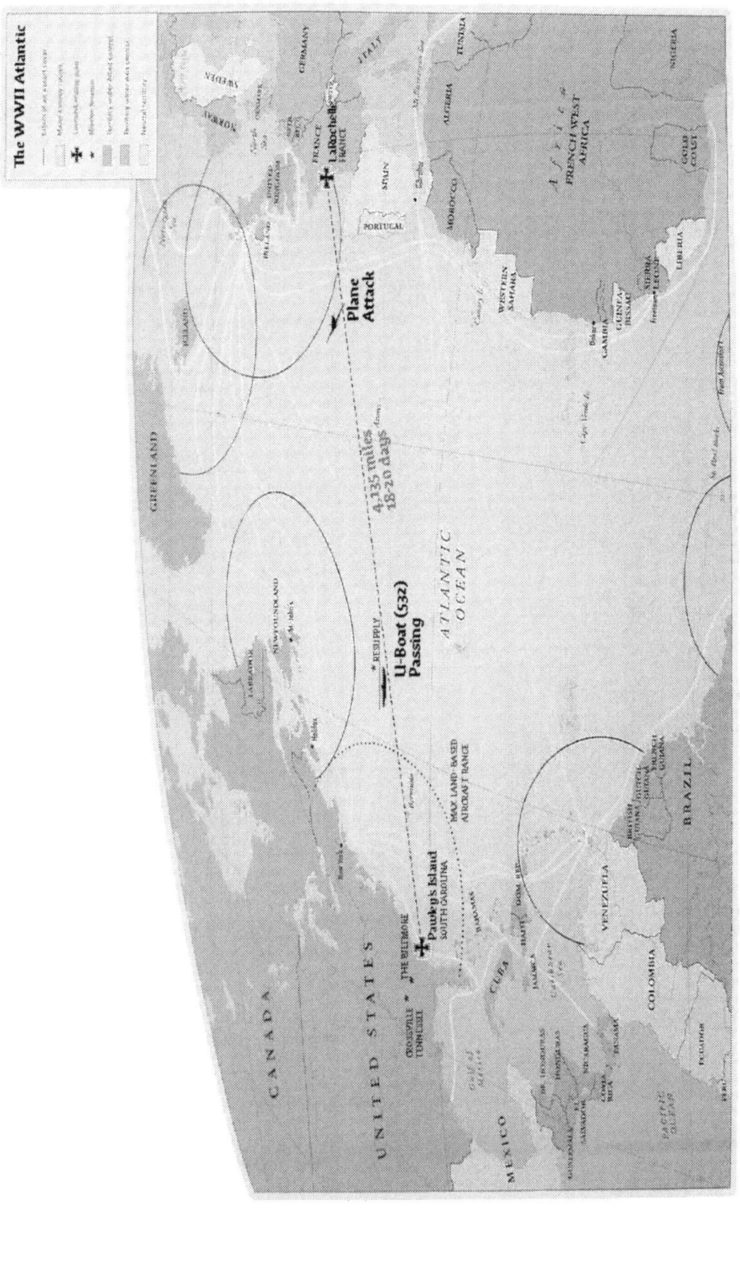
The WWII Atlantic
La Rochelle
FRANCE
Plane Attack
4,135 miles
18-20 days
RESUPPLY
U-Boat (532)
Passing
ATLANTIC
OCEAN
MAX LAND-BASED
AIRCRAFT RANGE
THE BILTMORE
Pawley's Island
SOUTH CAROLINA
CROSSVILLE
TENNESSEE
CANADA
UNITED STATES
MEXICO
GREENLAND
NEWFOUNDLAND
PORTUGAL
SPAIN
FRANCE
GERMANY
ITALY
SWEDEN
NORWAY
MOROCCO
ALGERIA
TUNISIA
FRENCH WEST
AFRICA
WESTERN
SAHARA
LIBERIA
NIGERIA
VENEZUELA
COLOMBIA
BRAZIL
CUBA

SIX

LA ROCHELLE, FRANCE
NOVEMBER 14, 1941

The tri-motored Junkers Ju 88 taxied up to the airport hangar, its aluminum skin rattling. After the steps were lowered, a corporal boarded. "Captain Gunther? Headquarters sent me to drive you to the base."

The corporal helped Gunther, Krauss, and Hellwig, all of whom were in civilian attire, load their gear and the special backpack into the waiting Opel. He drove them directly to the piers. The Navy had set up flak guns and guard posts to defend them. They went through three checkpoints before they reached the massive bunkers. Gunther and the other two marveled at the bulk and scale of the five thick shelters leading into the harbor. Construction was still underway on two more shelters. Bombs won't break through that concrete, thought Gunther.

Humping their gear, they crossed the gangway. Gunther showed his orders to the petty officer on watch, who sent a seaman below to get the commander.

Korvettenkapitan Ernst Bauer clambered up the ladder to the deck. Not being in uniform, Gunther came to attention. He dipped his head. "Sir, Captain Gunther, Lieutenant Krauss, and Sergeant Hellwig are reporting in accordance with travel plans previously conveyed to you." Gunther guessed Bauer must have just returned from his final briefing with the base commander. He was wearing dress blues. Gunther took in his medals. The U-boat Warfare Badge, the submarine Combat Clasp in Gold, and a combat wound badge in black. Probably rare in the submarine force, he thought. Most impressive was the Knight's Cross of the Iron Cross with Oak Leaf Cluster. Gunther's confidence in his upcoming voyage was slightly improved.

"Welcome aboard U-127, Herr Gunther. We intend to make this pleasant and swift despite the pesky British. You and Krauss will be hot bunking in the officer's quarters, such as they are. Sergeant Hellwig will be hot bunking with the general crew in the forward torpedo room. We don't have enough space for the sergeant in the petty officer's quarters. This boat carries four officers and forty-seven enlisted. Space is precious, as you will see from the foodstuffs we have packed into every open space. We filled the forward head from deck to ceiling with sacks of potatoes, so that head will be out of commission until halfway through our trip. We even have dry goods stored in one of the torpedo tubes."

Bauer, in turn, appraised Gunther; before him was a young man of average height, light brown hair, and a slight build who looked more like a college student than a military man. Moving on to Krauss; taller than Gunther, looked like a solid athlete, more like a military man. Hellwig was typical Nordic, blond, long-faced, and much skinnier than the others.

Gunther said, "We appreciate whatever you can provide, Kapitan. We'll try to stay out of your way."

"Difficult on a U-boat." Bauer nodded to an older man in coveralls. "Chief Hausch here will stow your gear."

"We'll keep this backpack with us."

"Fine. Now, the schedule I received is tight. We'll cast off in thirty minutes. When we're at diving stations, or if we're attacked, climb into the nearest bunk and stay there until you hear the All-Clear. Follow me."

Thirty minutes later, with Bauer and Gunther standing in the conning tower, the U-boat pulled out. Five sailors stood on deck behind the conning tower as the U-boat emerged from the bunker, a stubby harbor tug lashed alongside to pull her away from the pier extending between the bunkers. Seagulls lined the pier, watching for anything that might be tossed or dropped into the water. Sailors on the deck of an incoming U-boat waved to them.

Three hours later, they had traveled only forty-seven kilometers.

After their first three hours at sea, including a test dive, Gunther and the other Luftwaffe men had already learned that U-boat life was difficult. The narrow Krupp Steel tube was hot, loud, oily, smelly, and cramped. Uniforms and rank seemed to carry little significance. Half the crew went about bare-chested, and the others, even the officers, wore only undershirts.

The enlisted galley was a table swung down on chains. The crew had to eat in shifts or on their bunks. The officer's mess table could only accommodate four.

The Kapitan surfaced the boat and sent a seaman to ask Gunther if he wanted to come topside. Climbing an inner trunk to the conning station, Gunther felt the light saltwater spray hit his face. He tasted it on his lips. It was cold, and he wasn't dressed for the weather. He glanced around to see a forward lookout. Continuing his sweep, he saw an aft lookout. Both were scanning the sky and sea with binoculars. Behind him stood the XO, also scanning. Bauer clapped him on the back. "Now we're shipmates, Luftwaffe *Kameraden!* We're at the outer limits of where the damn Brit planes can hassle us. So, we stay on our toes up here! We can travel about 650 kilometers in twenty-four hours, surfaced. But only about 285 kilometers a day submerged. We can stay down, running off our batteries, for about forty-eight hours."

"How many patrols have you made?"

Suddenly, the aft lookout shouted, "Aircraft, starboard!"

Bauer and the executive officer, whom the crew called the "XO," whipped their binoculars to starboard. "Wellington! Alarm! Clear the bridge! Everyone below!" shouted the Kapitan.

Gunther followed the Executive Officer down the ladder and got out of the way, finding an unoccupied bunk. The lookouts and the Kapitan quickly slid down the ladder, slamming and dogging the hatch. Bauer yelled, "Dive! Dive! Make your depth 150 meters, left full rudder!"

At least a dozen crew members rushed to the bow of the boat to shift trim and dive faster.

As the submarine passed 75 meters, the sonarman yelled, "Depth charge." An explosion caused the boat to shake violently. It tossed Hellwig out of his bunk, glass from gauges shattered. A water leak sprayed aft of the petty officer's quarters. The crew swiftly plugged and sealed it. The submariners didn't speak. The boat grew quiet as they glided on. To Gunther's relief, no additional explosions followed.

After another fifteen minutes, the Kapitan said, "All Clear." A seaman told Gunther and his men they could move about once more. The Kapitan said, "Have Herr Gunther come to the control room."

In the control room, Bauer, standing over the map table, said, "We're about 125 kilometers west of Coruna, Spain. The Wellingtons can't usually make it out this far. This one must have fitted one of its bomb bay spaces with an extra fuel tank. That's why it only dropped one depth charge.

"So far, the British aren't accurate with their bombs. We hope that inaccuracy continues. We'll surface again in a couple of hours. We'll be well outside their range then and in the open Atlantic."

* * *

Gunther went to look for Hellwig and Krauss. He found Krauss standing outside the radio room, talking to a petty officer. "You okay?"

"I'm fine, but I'm not sure I can take much more of this kind of action."

"Check to see if our package was damaged."

He continued to the forward torpedo room. The U-boat designers had nestled the bunks above and around the torpedoes. Seeing two torpedomen, but not Hellwig, he went aft, passing the galley, the officer's quarters, the radio/sonar room and the petty officer's berthing, the engine room, and the ladder to the control room. No sign of Hellwig. He continued through the electric motor room and back into the aft torpedo room. Still no sign of the man.

Puzzled, Gunther backtracked to the forward torpedo room and started a more thorough search. He found the sergeant curled into a ball under a rack of torpedoes next to the bulkhead. Squatting next to Hellwig, Gunther shook him. Was he injured? Seeing no visible wounds, he asked, "What's wrong?"

Hellwig murmured, "I'm sorry, Captain, I can't handle this. I'm afraid I'm going crazy. I'm ashamed to admit I've considered slashing my wrists."

Gunther was unsure how to respond. "It'll get better, Sergeant. Stay here. I'll be back in a moment."

Gunther found the commander in the control room at the plotting table. "Do you have a second, Kapitan?" He gave him a brief description of the problem. The skipper nodded and said, "This sometimes happens. Let's find the hospitalman and see what he can prescribe." Speaking to the control room personnel, he said, "XO has the conn!"

"I have control," replied the XO.

Bauer took Gunther to the hospitalman's station. The medic said, "Sounds like claustrophobia. I'll give you some anti-anxiety pills. That should do for now. Give him two a day for a week, then one a day for a week, then one every other day until these are used up."

"Understand. Thanks."

Once back forward, he gave Hellwig the pills. Hellwig took two, and Gunther explained the schedule and suggested he lie in the bunk for a while.

Afterward, Gunther returned to tell Krauss what had transpired. Later, after lunch, he went back to check on Hellwig again. He was sleeping, as were the off-watch crew members. Gunther woke him and asked if he'd been to the galley.

"No, sir, but I don't feel as anxious. I'll try to eat something."

"Don't forget to take those pills."

"Aye, aye, Cap'n," said Hellwig, attempting a feeble joke.

* * *

As Gunther walked forward past the petty officer compartment, he saw a crewman pouring alcohol on a rag and rubbing himself down. "Chief, did you spill something on yourself?"

"No, sir, fresh water's too precious. We don't bathe when we're underway, just wipe ourselves down with alcohol. Then, we use cologne to mask the smell. We all smell like ladies of the night."

"I didn't know that. What else do you do that might be unique to U-boat duty?"

"Well, sir, the patrols can get monotonous, so we have our sing-a-longs, card games, like Skat, checkers, and chess, and our liars' competition."

"I've not heard of that, either."

"Oh, yes, sir. I've won it three times. Once, when I was actually telling a true secret."

"What was your true secret, Chief?"

"Well, sir, the Navy doesn't know this, but I'm the secret love child of Eleanor Roosevelt and Grand Admiral Raeder. Of course, he was only a lieutenant then. He was a naval aide at the Washington embassy. I keep it quiet because they'd try to make me an officer if they found out."

Gunther couldn't help but break into a grin. "Hell, Chief, you deserved to win! Could you do me a favor and have a crew member monitor Sergeant Hellwig? If he doesn't get up to eat, let me know so I can take him some chow."

"Will do it personally, sir," a rumble sounded from aft.

"How fast do you think we're going, Chief?"

"About fifteen knots, sir. The boat runs about two and a half times faster on the surface than we do submerged.

This is because, on the surface, we run on diesel engines, and when submerged, we run on lower horsepower electrical batteries." "Thanks, Chief. I may need that cologne in a day or two."

* * *

Krauss joined Gunther in the wardroom. Gunther studied the bird-watching guide, an integral part of their cover story. He switched to reviewing the op plan with Krauss. Hellwig, appearing doped, showed up and sat with them.

They studied the sketches Krauss had made during his student years at Chapel Hill. Gunther was viewing the large house's rear, the west side of the house. Having looked at drawings of the three other sides, he was now trying to envision where the Americans would place guards. Roving patrols would require his team to approach points differently than fixed posts. He'd not know how many personnel would be involved. He couldn't see how he'd get in if there were four posts. Looking again at the rear-view layout, he asked Krauss, "What's this small shape on the southwest of the drawing?"

Krauss searched through his pile of drawings and found the basement schematic. "Uh…that's a maintenance crawlway to the bowling alley."

Gunther recalled the details Goring had forwarded: something about Vanderbilt, his valet, and a hidden stairway running from the bowling alley to the valet's room on the fourth floor.

"We just might have an entry plan," he said. "A lot depends on where they post their guards. Let's keep looking. I don't think we should carry your drawings ashore, Werner. We might have trouble explaining them if we were searched. Memorize them, and we'll leave them with Bauer."

On the eighth night, while running on the surface, they received a radio message from U-532 saying they would pass five kilometers off U-127's port side as they headed home from their patrol area.

The remaining fourteen days of the trip across the Atlantic were uneventful, to the point of being monotonous.

The three did listen to a couple of the Liar's Competitions. They became convinced that the Luftwaffe could never top the Navy in the telling of falsehoods.

PAWLEY'S ISLAND, SOUTH CAROLINA
NOVEMBER 27, 1941

At 0300, U-127 slowly surfaced a rifle shot from the shoreline. Standing beside Bauer atop the conning tower, Gunther strained to listen for obstacles or activity. The U-boat moved silently forward. All he heard was the ocean lapping against the bulbous steel hull.

On this starry night, visibility was excellent. He could see a light in a house on the beach. On the forward deck, the front hatch flipped open. Two crewmen pushed a deflated rubber dinghy out onto the deck. They slowly pumped it up and slid it over the side, tying off a line to a recessed cleat to keep the dinghy from floating away.

Krauss and Hellwig climbed out of the forward hatch. They loaded their gear and some sausages and cheese the cook had provided. Krauss was wearing the special backpack with the painting.

Bauer said, "Do you know America well?"

"I've been here a half-dozen times. You?"

"Only once. The Yankees seem to be a trusting lot. That should help you. Good luck."

"I'll see you in four weeks." He shook Bauer's hand and swung down from the conning tower to the forward deck, where he handed his backpack to Hellwig and jumped down into the rocking dinghy.

Krauss untied the tether, and the three pushed off from the side as the submarine slowly motored away. The wind had increased, and waves broke over the sides of the dinghy, drenching them and their gear as they slowly paddled toward shore.

Once ashore, they fixed their bearing based on the position of the town's water tower, easily visible in the starry night. They pulled the dinghy up onto the sand and over a dune. Gunther would not be using it again; they were leaving at a different pickup point, and he didn't want to chance it being uncovered by anyone if he buried it in the sand. Using the American-made folding knife he'd requested, Gunther slashed the dinghy's air cells, deflating it.

The three set off for Beach Drive, with Gunther and Hellwig carrying the wadded-up bundle of heavy, wet rubber. At this hour, no one was out, and only one house had a light on. No cars were out. They were sweating in their heavy coats, but Gunther figured when they got to the hills of Tennessee, it would be a lot colder, and they would be thankful for the heavy clothing.

After trudging inland for a block, they found Beach Drive. Starting down the wrong way, they reversed course and soon found 313. He'd planned to store the deflated dinghy under a crawl space or in a basement. It surprised them when they saw the house was built on pilings.

Hellwig and Krauss crouched under a carport behind a sedan while Gunther climbed the steps to the front porch.

He found the key under the flower pots, just where they'd expected it. He opened the door and snapped his fingers, motioning the others to carry the dinghy inside.

There was no electricity. Hellwig retrieved a flashlight from his backpack. They stored the sandy, wet, deflated dinghy in a bedroom. They checked the kitchen and found the car key hanging on a hook.

Gunther told them to eat a small meal of canned fish, cheese, and bread. Then, they should rinse their clothes in the tub, wrap them in blankets, and step on them to draw out most of the moisture. "Don't forget to rinse the saltwater from your body."

With his flashlight, Gunther swept the house. He found shaving gear, soap, and safety razors in the medicine cabinet. On the submarine, they'd had no opportunity to bathe or shave. He took his pile to the kitchen sink, "Beards aren't that popular here; we should all shave while we have a chance. Then let's try to get some rest. It'll be daylight soon, and we'll leave this evening. Krauss, check the painting again."

Krauss carefully removed the painting from his special backpack and peeled back two layers of waterproofing and cushioning. He checked the front and back of Goring's copy. "I believe she has come through undamaged. A little soggy around the wrappings, but she's fine. I'll dry the wrapping."

They found some stale coffee and lit the gas stove. Gunther sat them down with their coffee mugs and said, "We're on foreign soil now. Germany is not at war with the United States; however, we are, at a minimum, illegal aliens. Since we're not breaking laws or carrying weapons, maybe we won't be charged as spies if we get discovered."

* * *

Eleven hours later, as night fell, they heated cans of Campbell's beans Hellwig found in a cupboard. Then, they loaded their backpacks into the Ford sedan. But nothing happened when Gunther turned the key and stepped on the starter. He tried three times. Finally, he turned the headlights on. They wouldn't work either. "Dead battery," said Gunther. He sat there momentarily. "Nothing to do but steal one."

He rolled out with one of their flashlights and opened the hood. "I'll need a wrench." Krauss looked behind the rear seat and found tools wrapped in a cloth pouch bearing the Ford Motor Company logo.

After waiting another hour to ensure everyone was in bed, they removed the battery. After taking the wrench and dead battery with them, Hellwig and Krauss searched for a battery from another car. They wanted another Ford so the owners wouldn't know someone had switched batteries. Finding another under a house a block away, they quietly switched. Returning to Gunther and the sedan, they bolted in the stolen battery. They got in, and Gunther hit the starter again.

By 0100, they were headed for Darlington, North Carolina, then on to Asheville, then over the mountains to Knoxville, and then Crossville, Tennessee.

Seventy-five miles later, according to the odometer, the gas gauge read near empty, and Gunther noticed steam around the radiator cap. They pulled into an Esso station. It was still an hour before it would open. They took a leak in the weeds behind it. After it opened, the attendant filled up the tank and added water to the radiator. "Hey, Mac! You let your car sit for too long. The tires are all low, and the right rear has a flat spot. Also, your radiator hose is about to burst. You want me to fix this?"

"Air the tires. We'll get it fixed when we get to where we're going."

"Ok. I'd at least buy an extra radiator hose to have with me in the car."

After paying for the gas and buying a spare hose, Krauss told Gunther, "Since we're students at Chapel Hill and on our way to visit family in Knoxville, perhaps I should be driving."

"I agree; besides, you've probably driven in North Carolina before."

"Oh, yes. We should plan on getting about two hundred American miles, or a little more, from a full tank."

Twenty minutes later, in Matthews, Krauss noticed a police car following them. After another three minutes, the sheriff turned on his big red roof light and pulled them over.

As the officer walked up, he found the driver's window rolled down. "South Carolina plates, boys?"

"Yes, sir," said Krauss/Jonathon Turner. "I borrowed the car from my roommate at UNC."

"These plates is expired," said the sheriff. "Where you boys headed?"

"My classmates and I are headed to Knoxville for Christmas with my uncle and his family."

The grossly overweight sheriff was wearing a plaid shirt, worn dress pants, and a straw cowboy hat. His badge was pinned to his shirt pocket, and he wore a holstered revolver on his left hip. His shoes were scuffed, and Krauss could swear he was wearing mismatched socks.

The sheriff looked at the car and asked Gunther/Seth Brown, "You from around here, Bubba?"

"No, officer, I'm from Toledo. This is also my last year at school. Can't wait to get a job and start a family." He sounded casual, but Gunther wondered if he could detect his accent.

The sheriff had glanced only once at Hellwig/Chris Wagg. Luckily, he didn't ask him a question. Looking the car over again, he finally said, "Have your buddy get those new license plates real soon."

"Will do, Sheriff," said Krauss/Turner. "Merry Christmas!"

"You, too," said the sheriff.

* * *

Pulling back onto the road, Krauss loudly exhaled. "Well, that could have been worse," he said in English. "I never thought to look at the plates, especially in the dark! Crap, it could have not even had plates on it. That would have put us in a real pickle. Worse, what would we have done if he'd tried to arrest us?"

"We couldn't have allowed that," said Gunther. "As a last resort, be prepared to defend our mission by violence if need be. We should purchase a baseball bat, ball, and glove. I can use the bat as a weapon."

They drove on and were soon southwest of Charlotte. The following two hours seemed to take days. Another hour and they would pass south of Asheville. They stopped to fuel up again. Krauss said, "The route from this point on will be the road we'll be doubling back on after leaving Crossville with Muller."

Past Asheville, the mountains grew much steeper. According to the map, the distance from Asheville to Crossville was approximately one hundred fifty miles.

Krauss was getting exhausted. The other two had caught some sleep during the drive.

Gunther said they'd switch drivers in Tennessee.

In Knoxville, Gunther stopped again to get gas. He bought a baseball bat, glove, and ball. He studied their Standard Oil map. He found a state park with an adjoining hunting range just six kilometers outside Crossville. They decided to stop and rest there before scouting the camp and devising a plan to contact Lieutenant Muller.

Muller worked at Thomas Teas's Dairy Farm, three kilometers north of the prisoner of war camp. The Consulate had even learned that Muller worked each Monday, Wednesday, and Friday, but they didn't know what job he performed.

While getting gas at a well-stocked country store, they purchased canned potatoes, beef, bread, cheese, and sausage. They also bought a box of tea bags but doubted they'd be able to build a fire once they reached the Estate. The back floorboard was filled with enough food to sustain them for four or five days. Gunther figured they would have to do this same thing again just before reaching Biltmore.

SEVEN

BILTMORE
NOVEMBER 29, 1941

Donahue was finishing up a letter to Alaina Avara. In her last letter, she'd asked if there was any chance he could get time off at Christmas. He replied that he missed her dearly, but Christmas leave wouldn't happen for him. Others in the detail were taking off, and they needed him here more than ever.

Knocking on the open door frame, Joseph stepped in. "Is the desk still wobbly?"

"A little, but I've got a piece of cardboard under it. Is it getting colder?"

"Much. I can get to the repair now if you'd like. The crate's finished. Would you like to take a look?"

"Can't wait."

The finished piece sat on the shop floor. The contrast between the many pieces of exotic wood veneer and its massive size made it hard for him to take his eyes off the custom-built puzzle crate.

The finished product is a museum piece in its own right, thought Donahue. "Truly amazing!"

"*Spasiba*, Captain."

"How heavy do you think it is?"

"With the painting, it might be around 125-135 kilos, or 275-300 pounds. Much too heavy for me to add any incline style opening sequences."

"That's what I had in mind. One of the reasons I wanted this design was that I did not want any protrusions. Handles, or anything like that, would assist someone in picking it up and making off with it. I want it to be hard to move by anything less than three men."

"I added forty opening sequences and a few tricks from European boxes. I believe those were German-made. The major addition requires a magnet to reveal and open certain drawers in the sequence. I could have embedded the magnet in a drawer to be opened just before the magnet is needed. But, because of the value of the painting being stored, I felt it required a stricter usage of the magnet." Joseph displayed a magnet roughly 4" long by 2" thick. "Let me show you how to open the sixty-four steps."

He went through the sequences twice. Donahue tried but got hung up at sequence number thirty.

"Let me go through it again," said Joseph.

Donahue tried again and got through step forty-five.

Joseph showed him the steps from where he was stuck.

After reassembling the box, Donahue was successful on his third try.

"That's difficult and takes some time," said Donahue. "If you don't work this thing regularly, you'll forget some of those steps. This is terrific. I'll put in a government chit to pay you."

"Not necessary, Captain, but appreciated."

"I'll have my men move it to the third floor. We can use the elevator. The men can use the stairs, wait to unload, then move the box to the Living Hall. There are many turns in the corridor walking from the elevator on the north side. I've measured each turn. We can make it without damaging the crate or the walls, but I'll throw blankets over it to be safe."

The enlisted men left after moving the crate to its new location. Donahue, Phillipe, and Maurice admired it.

Daniel Roberts stood to the side, looking befuddled. "The...Mona Lisa is going in...there?"

"Unless you object, sir. Then you can try to access it, ok? That would be a good test. After Mr. Buchard gets up, he and I will load it. Have him find me when he's ready."

* * *

Donahue was eating wiener schnitzel and red potatoes with the staff in their basement eating area when one of the cooks said to a maid, "I saw Mrs. Cecil and the boys leaving early this morning. I heard the chauffeur say they might not return."

Randolph, who also heard this, said simply, "Ladies."

The cook switched subjects: "Did you know Miss Schneider quit? She moved to the West Coast. Must have gotten a job in the new airplane plants there. I hated to see her leave. She was one of the few girls with a sense of humor."

At that moment, Buchard came in. After wiping his mouth with his napkin, Donahue, rising to leave, said to Randolph, "Compliment Mrs. Thatcher for me, please."

Turning to Buchard, Donahue said, "Have you seen our little project?"

They headed for the stairs. "As fine a piece of woodcraft as I've seen."

"Ready to load?"

"Show me how to open it, and we'll slide her in. I tried to move the box, but it's impossible with just two of us."

"That was the idea," said Donahue.

When they reached the Living Hall and pushed aside one of the heavy entry curtains, the smiling lady reclined beside the puzzle crate on an easel, still uncrated from her test fitting.

Buchard asked the other Frenchmen, "Phillipe, can you and Maurice give us a few moments?"

"Certainly, Antoine."

"I'm afraid I must ask you to leave as well, Mr. Roberts," said Donahue.

"These are National Gallery artworks, Captain."

"True enough, sir. But the item we're working with is strictly the property of France."

Roberts, looking uncertain, said, "Of course, Captain. I agree."

* * *

After they left, Donahue showed Buchard the magnet and reviewed the opening sequences until the crate opened. Reversing the sequences, they closed the exotic crate, then Buchard tried opening it. He needed some assistance, but after executing the process twice more, he had it memorized.

Donahue asked, "May I inspect the Mona Lisa before we slide her in?"

"Of course," said Buchard while moving the easel to the corner of the room. While Buchard was doing this, Donahue took a straight pin he'd stuck in his uniform tie and pricked the bottom right corner of the wood backing. This had been a part of his and the master sergeant's security plan. He stuck the pin back in his tie. Buchard returned, and they loaded the painting into its compartment and reassembled the crate.

Donahue said, "Let's try to move the crate around."

They tried. Because of the prosthetic arm, he had to try to push with his shoulder. Using all their might, they managed to scoot it about two feet. "Good," said Donahue.

Buchard placed the magnet in his desk drawer and locked it with a key on his treasured watch fob.

He called Roberts, Phillipe, and Maurice back in, and Buchard and Donahue started toward Donahue's office. "Mr. Roberts, give the crate another shot if you'd like."

Donahue asked Buchard, "Any changes or additions you'd like to make or add to the security plan while your compatriots are on leave?"

"I believe what we have in place will be sufficient," said Buchard, "Have a good evening, Captain. You know where I'll be from 8 p.m. to 8 a.m. if you need me."

TEAS'S DAIRY FARM
CROSSVILLE, TENNESSEE
DECEMBER 2, 1941

On Tuesday, Gunther, Krauss, and Hellwig rested at the hunting preserve for the day. The next morning, they parked as close to the farm as seemed safe. From there, lying in the grass with their binoculars, they watched the POWs being unloaded from a U.S. Army deuce-and-a-half truck. Gunther pointed out Muller, but the others had already noticed the Hellwig look-alike.

They observed for the entire day. It appeared Muller's job was to feed the cattle after they'd been milked. The cattle were mostly black and white, but about a third were red and white. Gunther had seen these in Germany. He thought they were Holsteins and Jerseys. While most of the workers labored inside the massive barns, Muller and three other POWs toiled outside. The outside workers had to make trips back and forth between the barns. They herded the cows outside after milking to feed on the haystacks they'd built with pitchforks. Since the cows had also been fed before milking, some ate from the stacks again at this time, while others just drifted farther from the barns. They moved closer to a dozen goats that were grazing under a trio of old oaks. A large black dog playfully ran back and forth between the goats and the cattle.

Gunther and the others caught a whiff of cow manure and fresh paint fumes as the wind shifted.

Around three in the afternoon, the deuce-and-a-half returned and loaded the POWs for the trip back to camp. Gunther and the other two sneaked away to the hunting preserve for the night.

Krauss said while eating cold canned sausage, bread, and beer, "I can't believe they left only one guard for eleven PWs, and he spent all his time sitting in the doorway of one barn, talking to two children…is it me, or is American beer very weak?"

They argued about American beer, then Hellwig lit up a U.S. Chesterfield and, in German, said, "We need to buy some more cigarettes; I'm almost out. I can't believe I went all day without a ciggie. The life of a POW doesn't seem to be rough at all at this camp."

Gunther said, "We'll contact Muller on Friday. We must tell him about the plan to switch on Monday. We can't send Hellwig to talk to him; if they were seen, it'd be like having a set of twins to explain. I'll go."

"Won't they see you," asked Krauss.

"Most of those haystacks are taller than a man," said Gunther. "I'll approach, keeping the haystacks between me and the MP. I'll quickly tell him how he and Hellwig will change clothes and switch places. I'll ask what the routine is for Hellwig back at the barracks. I'll also ask him who his buddies are back there. It'll help Hellwig get through the first few days of acting."

* * *

On Friday, they returned to their viewing spot. They waited until Muller and the others brought their second herd to the stacks. Keeping Muller and a haystack between him and the guard, Gunther crept up. As he got close, Muller was startled. Gunther placed his finger to his lips. "It's me, Conrad! Rolf Gunther. I have to speak quickly."

"Rolf?" said Muller. "*Oh, mein lieber Gott!* What are you doing here?"

Gunther shushed him again. "Listen! Monday morning, we're switching you out with a soldier who looks like you. First, you'll change clothes with him. Make one of your hay stacks twelve centimeters taller than it is now, and be sure to work on this side of the stack. Tonight, tell someone you trust you'll be leaving, and the one replacing you will need his help to learn the routine. I'll explain the rest after you're freed. I've got to go now. See you Monday, my friend."

With that, Gunther, again using the haystack for concealment, crawled back out of the field to rejoin Krauss and Hellwig.

CROSSVILLE, TENNESSEE
DECEMBER 4, 1941

Gunther, Krauss, and Hellwig spent the weekend discussing the plan. Early Monday, they drove to the farm, parked, and crept to their surveillance spot, watching as

Muller and the others brought their second herd out to graze.

Hellwig, emulating the creep-and-dash tactics Gunther had used Friday, swiftly made his way to Muller's side. Once there, he and Muller rapidly began pulling their clothing off.

The swap was taking longer than Gunther had expected. He kept his binoculars on the guard, a slim youngster around eighteen years old, who now and then glanced toward the haystacks. He must have been concerned that only three POWs could be seen working. He finally rose from his stool and started walking toward where he expected to see Muller. As he got halfway to Muller's haystack, one of the POWs, the one Muller must have confided in, Gunther guessed, fell to the ground and yelled, "*Hilf mir!* I've broken my ankle!"

The MP looked at the fallen POW, then back at Muller's haystack, hesitating, but continued toward the stack. Even more quickly now, Hellwig finished changing. He grabbed the pitchfork and began tossing fresh hay to the top of the stack.

Upon seeing hay flying, the MP turned back to check on the man who'd called for help.

Muller crawled toward Gunther, keeping the haystack between him and the MP.

Creeping away toward their car, Gunther thought, *It's up to Hellwig now. Hope he doesn't screw this up.*

* * *

As Krauss drove from Crossville toward Asheville, Gunther introduced Muller to Krauss. "When you've caught your breath, I'll tell you what's going on."

Muller took a deep breath. "Why would The Reich bother to get me out of a POW camp? How is the war going? Does my family know where I am or if I'm alive? How is my darling, Katerina?"

Gunther answered Muller's questions as best he could, then said, "We switched Sergeant Hellwig with you because you have knowledge that's valuable to our mission. We're here to switch a copy of the Mona Lisa for the real thing. The real Mona Lisa is currently at the Biltmore Estate in Asheville. We have what Reichsmarschall Goring says is an exact copy, and he wants the original."

Muller sat in silence for a moment. After digesting all this, he said, "Then, it must be a Chaudron copy. Can I look at it?"

"After we go over the plan," said Gunther. He then told Muller the entire story, beginning with his beckoning to Goring's office. He ended with, "I'm sure you have many questions."

"I do, but first, when we get a chance, I'd like to see the copy."

* * *

When they crossed the North Carolina state line, Gunther told Krauss to pull over at the next public picnic area.

Once they had pulled off, Muller asked to use a flashlight even though it was daylight.

"Oh, sure," said Gunther. He got out and retrieved one from behind the seats.

He returned to the front seat and noticed a large *Whites Only* sign beside a picnic table. That reminded him of a *Nein Juden* sign he'd seen at the Berlin Zoo.

Krauss slid the painting from his backpack and handed it over. Muller delicately unwrapped it from its waterproof coverings and looked at it in the sunlight for several minutes. He then used the flashlight to check small details as if against some checklist in his memory. Muller then spent several minutes looking at the reverse and the frame. Finally, he whistled.

"It's wonderful. I question the frame, but the original's been repaired and replaced at least two times, probably more. Only a true expert, like Antoine Buchard, could say whether it's incorrect."

Gunther and Krauss smiled at each other. Gunther said, "He'll get his chance."

"How so?"

"Buchard's also at the Biltmore." He went on to explain in more detail how the *Mona Lisa* and Buchard had wound up in the U.S. And how they'd coerced Buchard into assisting them in this mission.

Muller continued to admire the painting. He said to no one in particular, "My post-graduate degree thesis was on the artwork of Leonardo da Vinci. He painted La Gioconda on a poplar panel."

"For all her storied history, I'd expected her to be larger," said Krauss.

"She's average-sized for a portrait of that era. An Italian stole her from the Louvre, and she remained missing for over two years before the museum got her back. During that hiatus, a master forger named Yves Chaudron created six high-quality copies. This is obviously one. The work is truly breathtaking."

"Have you ever seen another copy?" asked Gunther.

"Yes, I've seen one other Chaudron. The Louve had one donated, and they occasionally displayed it alongside the original. I believe this is slightly better than the one I saw."

"Have you met Buchard?" asked Krauss.

"Once, at a lecture on art preservation. I also attended a lecture by another professor who spoke on what it would take for someone to do a realistic copy of the Mona Lisa. The artist must know da Vinci's unique techniques. He'd have to find a properly cured poplar panel and prepare it with traditional gesso, then hand-grind paint pigments in walnut oil. He'd likely start with an underdrawing and use many layers of transparent glazing. The darkness of the original varnish and the cracked glazing would be hard to reproduce realistically."

"Why haven't more artists done copies?" asked Gunther.

"It wouldn't be a task for the faint of heart. The reverse would be equally difficult. In some ways, more so, with the dovetail repairs inserted to keep the panel from twisting from the drying out of the poplar panel. To complete six copies in two years, Chaudron must have worked on all six simultaneously so the aging process would be the same. Amazing!"

Muller's knowledge reassured the other two officers. He rewrapped the painting as carefully as if it were an injured pet and returned it to Krauss's special backpack.

Gunther said, "Just before we stop for the evening, we'll stop to fill the tank and buy food to last a week. Any more questions about our objective, Conrad?"

"Not for now. Thank you for coming to get me."

BILTMORE
DECEMBER 5, 1941

Gunther had thought about where to park close to the Estate. The House was situated deep within the property. Aside from where tourists had parked before it was closed to the public, the nearest public parking was over a kilometer away. He'd settled on Bent Creek Public Park. It was ideally located alongside the French Broad River. He hoped it was not uncommon to leave cars there for days.

As Gunther walked around the park, he noted that the leaves of the deciduous trees had already fallen. Multicolored leaves covered the ground and all the walkways. Concrete picnic tables and benches were placed every twenty to thirty feet. The weather was getting cloudier, and though it was already cold, the temperature was dropping even more. Viewing the sparsely covered trees, he thought *our surveillance area would be exposed this time of the year. I hope the forest around Biltmore is mostly evergreens.*

Walking down to the river's edge, he found a few small skiffs for fishing or rowing tied up near a rental shack. A sign read *One Hour 25¢*, but no one was around. "These people are very trusting," Krauss said.

"It is a strange country," said Muller, "But this area reminds me of sections of the Rhine. My father and I used to fish there."

"This may work out to our advantage," said Gunther.

They returned to their car and retrieved their gear and the food. At the last moment, Gunther said, "Conrad, strap that bat to your pack." They then hiked back to the boats. Picking the sturdiest-looking, they loaded it. Finding no paddles, Hellwig broke the padlock on the shack and retrieved two. He also took a handful of Hershey bars from an open box. They hoped no one would search the river when the owner finally noticed the lock was broken and the boat and paddles missing.

Paddling up the French Broad, Krauss again commented, "This is exactly like the Rhine. See the green rolling hills on our left and the farmland on our right."

Gunther almost forgot they were on a mission. After three and a half kilometers farther, the team came to the Biltmore Lagoon.

He thought this would be an excellent place to hide the skiff. They pulled it into the wooded area separating the lagoon from the river and covered it with leaves and branches.

Having studied a map of Asheville, Gunther had decided the southwest approach, from the lagoon to the forest, would best surveil the House. They'd still need to find a clearer view of the northeast side. The northeast contained the stables, the carriage house, and the service entrance. They'd scout that area after finding an overall surveillance site.

From the lagoon, Gunther used the binoculars and located a sentry at the northeast end of the driveway. Continuing to scan to his left, he found another on a terrace at the south end of Biltmore House. This was the sentry they'd have to avoid as they entered.

They continued down the southeast side, through woods behind the large garden, and onto the rear of the house. After settling on a temporary site, they dropped their packs and food bundles. They unpacked the shelter halves and spread them on the ground.

Pointing to their packs, Gunther said to Muller, "As part of our planning, we had the New York Consulate purchase our clothing, these shelter halves, and all the other cover story items we needed. I'm afraid we can't count on having enough food. We'll have to improvise. We can go deeper into the woods and boil water from the lagoon."

The shelter halves were the only bedding and rainproof gear they carried. Had they been searched, their story on why they had shelter halves would have been that, as bird watchers, they occasionally spent the night outdoors. They were students with little extra money; they didn't rent motel rooms. The *Birds of America* book would explain the binoculars. Explaining the copy of the *Mona Lisa* would have been more challenging, but perhaps possible, given the cover story of one of them studying art at the University.

The air was colder here than it had been in Crossville. Gunther feared they could not stand too many days if it got much colder. He hoped it didn't.

Through the binoculars, he quickly identified two sentries. One was at the northern end of the house. A second was posted on the patio at the southern end. He'd have to scout out the front again to see if three was the number of sentry locations. He hoped that was all.

He focused on the southwest windows of the South Tower Room. The binoculars showed nothing posted there. He sent Muller and Krauss patrolling in opposite directions to scout any paths that might let someone stumble upon their position.

He planned to spend at most ten days here. But, if that wasn't the case, they had allotted double that. He hoped to spend the extra time closer to the ocean while waiting for the U-boat to return. Maybe even doing some ocean fishing. Why not? If the plan worked, no one would be looking for them. No one would even have a reason to suspect they weren't students on Christmas break.

He set up a schedule for one of them to watch the sentries and activity around the north end, where most movements seemed to occur. He showed Muller and Krauss how to cup their hands around the front of the lenses to prevent glare flashes from the rising sun in the morning. Any flash might be seen by one of the sentries.

On their second day on the overwatch, Krauss heard a sharp knock nearby. "Hey, didn't you hear that? What is it?"

Gunther listened, then smiled. "I only know this because I read the bird book on the U-boat. That is a woodpecker. It pecks on trees to find food, then eats using its beak to pull insects out of tree bark."

None of the Germans had ever heard this sound. They were just as surprised when they heard their first owl scream during the night.

On their third day, a heavy frost covered the ground. Gunther, his shelter-half held tightly around his shoulders, sat shivering and listening to the morning quietness of the woods. They hadn't slept that night. They'd all been much too cold. In addition to the terrible weather, Krauss told Gunther he thought he'd cracked a tooth while they were in Crossville. He believed it was infected. Gunther listened impatiently while checking the South Tower windows. There was no yellow sign.

"Keep me informed about the tooth."

Looking through the binoculars, Muller said, "The two sentries I can see are also shivering, but at least they're wearing watch caps. Also, I smell pork cooking. That must be the kitchen exhaust vent at our ten o'clock position. My stomach is going crazy."

"Try not to think about it," said Gunther.

BASEMENT

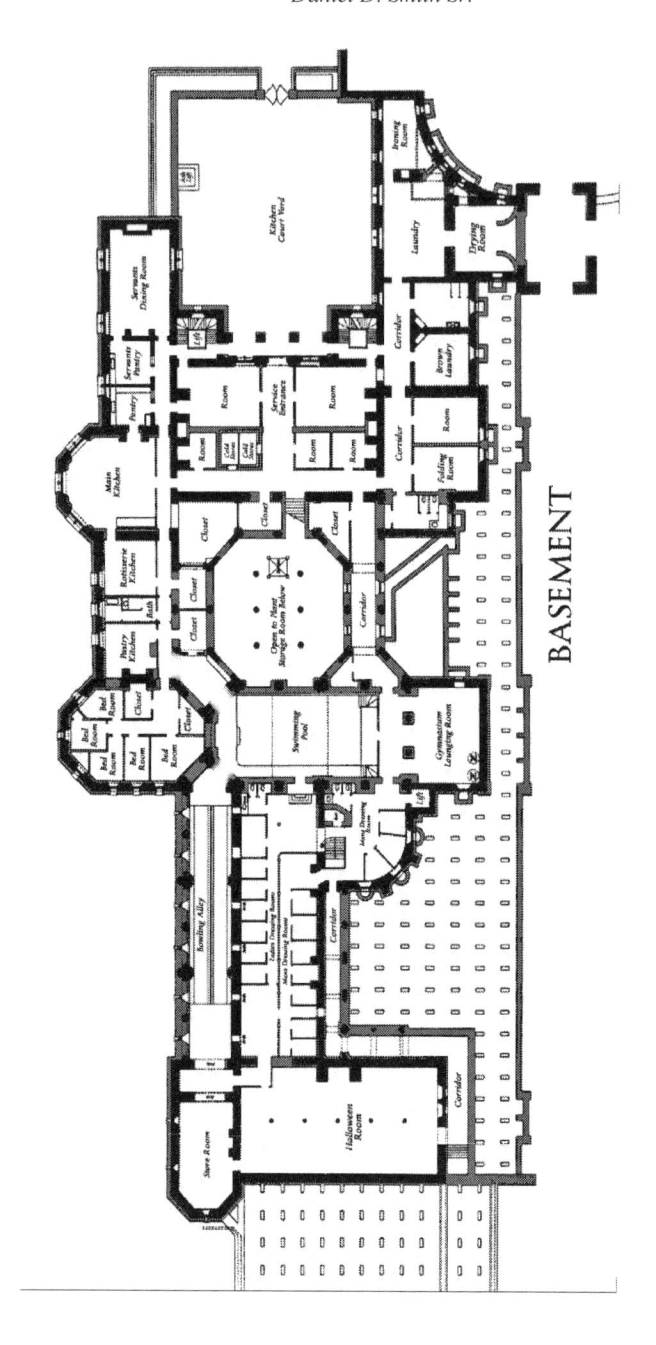

Periodically, he checked on the hidden boat. They'd be in real trouble if it wasn't there when they were ready to leave. Krauss took over the binoculars. Gunther sent Muller to check on the boat. Near the main gardens, Muller was almost discovered by a Biltmore gardener dumping raked leaves in a compost pile at the forest's edge.

Gunther felt they wouldn't survive another cold night. He discussed this with the others after Muller returned from the boat.

"Werner, what do you remember about the area around the bowling alley?"

"As you turn left coming out of the access door, there are two rooms on the left. You might find blankets there. Keep going to your left, and you'll find the main kitchen. There has to be food."

Gunther decided, *"I'll have to breach the house sooner than our plan called for."* He thought that if he didn't, they were likely to fail or have to leave if they wanted to survive.

At 0200, he slowly and quietly crept through the forest and into the more open grounds. Two dozen medium-sized firs grew between the house's north and south end. They weren't quite large enough to hide a man but were maybe large enough to disguise one. Any Luftwaffe man knew that the human eye detected movement better than anything else. He cautiously moved from tree to tree.

The last thirty meters to the abutment in the foundation were the most dangerous. There were no trees, just open ground. The northern sentry had a clear view of this field. The sentry at the south had his view restricted by the cut in the corner foundation. Apparently, the south sentry was tasked with covering both the house's rear and front. He seemed to patrol from the front of the Grand Patio to the backside of the terrace every thirty minutes, then switch positions again.

Gunther waited at the last tree concealment until the south sentry moved to the front of the Grand Patio. Glancing north, he saw that the northwest sentry was also looking north.

Fast crawling and keeping his eye on the north sentry, he quickly covered the thirty meters to the abutment. Beyond that, neither guard could see the entry grate to the maintenance tunnel.

The tunnel was more correctly a crawl space rather than a tunnel, but it was large enough to drag a workman's tool bag in and out. He and the special backpack made it through. Once through the short crawl space, he found a small hatch that opened directly next to one of the bowling lanes. Crawling through and pulling shut the hatch behind him, he blinked his flashlight briefly to orient himself.

To the left would be the stairway to Mr. Vanderbilt's bedroom, up past the second and on the fourth floor if he should choose to go that high. Next to the hidden stairway's entry would be the bedrooms of the House's junior staff. Some would be empty, but rather than chance going into a room with someone sleeping, he decided to search for linen closets.

Krauss had told him the floor plan showed four or five closets straight ahead from the bowling ball rack. After looking through the first three closets and not finding linens, Gunther found a pastry kitchen across from the closets. His beam illuminated trays of sweet muffins and a dozen loaves of bread. Going back to one of the closets, he removed a laundry sack. He stuffed in a half-dozen muffins and a loaf and continued his search.

He next found the main kitchen. To the right was a large pantry. Shelves held hundreds of canned goods. He took three cans of beans, two of corn, and four of what looked like small sausages.

Leaving the pantry and choosing a corridor he believed would take him to the other side of the basement, he found a room that had a small sign on the wall that read Folding Room. Glancing in, he saw linens and blankets. Wanting to stay with a dark theme, he wrapped a blanket around two more wool blankets and the white laundry sack. He also placed his empty backpack in this makeshift sack. Then he headed back past the indoor swimming pool. This would take him back to the bowling alley.

Suddenly, he heard movement in the kitchen area. He stepped behind the entrance to the locker room. Looking back past the bedrooms and the hallway running past the kitchen, he saw a light come on in the Pastry room. Of course, he thought, bakers always start their day in the middle of the night.

Gunther tiptoed back to the hatch in the bowling alley. He barely made it through the tight tunnel with his homemade sack. The canned goods rattled against each other. Those muffins are going to be in rough shape, he thought.

Outside, pausing to time his movements, Gunther slowly crawled from tree to tree. It reminded him of playing soldier in the woods with his childhood friend, Peter, when he was eight years old. He hoped both sentries were too far away to hear the sack dragging on the ground. Once past the small trees, he melded with the forest.

Relief spread through his body. Another three minutes and he was back at their surveillance site. He had Muller store the goods and told them to both have a sweet muffin. He told Krauss to soak his in water because of his tooth.

EIGHT

BILTMORE
DECEMBER 7, 1941

Captain Donahue sat at his desk, drinking coffee and reading the *Asheville Citizen/Times*. Gibbs was smoking at his table. His ashtray already held three butts from this morning. He was reading a draft Army field manual for military police operations. A fellow sergeant in D.C. had shared it with him. Gibbs had dove into it enthusiastically, believing it was a good match for his current duties.

"How's the watch rotation going? Any trouble with the 3-man shift?" asked Donahue.

"Going smoothly, Captain. No troubles, I can see. But I need to come up with more for the men to do off-watch. The guys are getting rowdy, and I had to break up a fight."

"I hope the boys enjoyed the shepherd's pie the kitchen sent out yesterday evening?"

"They sure did. I enjoyed adding some fresh beef to my diet. And, with apple cobbler topping it off, I felt like I was back home."

"Think we should review the security plan again?"

"Yes, sir. Is now a good time?" said Gibbs, setting aside his manual. "I've been thinking we should add an outer perimeter check to the plan. There are horses in the stables. Every day, I see a guy feeding and watering 'em. I've even seen an occasional brushing, but I've never seen anyone actually ride 'em. If you get permission, Gatlin and I could take them out. We could check the perimeter while also exercising the horses. Gatlin grew up in Texas. I grew up in Kentucky. As kids, both of us rode a lot."

"An excellent idea, Sergeant."

* * *

Finding John Cecil in the Oak Sitting Room, Donahue asked, "Do you have a moment, Mr. Cecil?"

"Call me John, Captain. How can I be of assistance?"

"Well, sir, we're thinking of adding a perimeter patrol to our security and would like to use a couple of your horses."

"I see." Cecil stroked his thin mustache. "Even though we seldom ride anymore, the horses are dear to me, Captain. They're almost a sensitive subject."

"Yes, sir. I understand. If I might add, not just anyone would be riding them. I have two men who were raised with horses. If it would help, I can have them relieve your staff and add daily maintenance of all the horses to their duties."

"That sounds acceptable, Captain. Can I meet these men?"

"Certainly, sir. In the stables, let's say, in an hour?"

"An hour will be fine, Captain."

Donahue told Gibbs to have himself and Gatlin standing by the horses in forty-five minutes.

"When do you want the first patrol, sir?" asked Gibbs.

"After we meet Cecil. There's plenty of daylight left. Tack's next to the stalls."

John Cecil met with Donahue, Gibbs, and Gatlin. After talking about the horses for a few minutes and giving them the animals' names, he shook their hands, then stepped into the carpenter's shop to talk with Joseph.

Looking at the fine horses, Gibbs chose Sheila, and Gatlin chose Vandy. They saddled them and rode out in the direction of the rear north sentry. They stopped momentarily and made sure Private Starks knew they'd be coming in and told him the password was "Phoenix." They also told him to pass it along to his relief, and that they'd give it to all the troops at morning formation.

* * *

Lieutenant Krauss, jaw swelling from his infected tooth, was at the binocular watch. He crawled back to the other two. "Captain, we may have a problem."

"What's going on?"

Two troopers are skirting the forest on horseback. They'll be here in minutes."

Gunther said, "Quickly, throw your shelter halves over your other equipment and get behind the small rise to our right. Maybe the shelter halves will blend in with the pines."

Behind the rise, the three Germans kept their heads down and concentrated on listening. "I wish we had rifles," Krauss muttered.

"This is not that kind of mission," Gunther hissed, "A little luck, detailed planning, and finesse will make this successful."

* * *

Every so often, as they patrolled the forest's edge, Gibbs and Gatlin turned to their right and rode into the woods for a few yards. Once inside the forest, the horses had to dodge scrub growth, and their riders had to duck low-hanging limbs. Vandy reared his head and snorted loudly. "See anything?" said Gibbs. "Shit, I can't see bupkus!" Gatlin pulled up Vandy and twisted in his saddle to look around more carefully. "No, I don't see anything. Want to ride deeper in?"

"I don't think so," said Gibbs. "We'll ask the carpenter how far this part of the forest goes."

Gibbs and Gatlin kept on at a slow trot around the forest's edge. They passed the lagoon. They continued for another 180 degrees before returning to the stable entrance by the front north sentry, where Gibbs gave the sentry the password.

"I'll unsaddle and brush," Gatlin said.

"I'll brief the captain," said Gibbs as he lit a cigarette.

Donahue was at his desk. "Back already? How'd that work out?"

"OK, Captain. I've got a better feel for the surroundings, and in my opinion, our posts are well placed."

"Very good. How often do you think we should make this outer sweep?"

"Um…maybe daily. I'd like to ask Joseph how deep the forest goes in the rear. Can you check with Mr. Cecil to see if he has any objection to that often?"

"Very well."

Donahue found Cecil in the library. "Do you have a moment, John?"

"Certainly, how'd the ride go? I could see the men from my study."

"It went well. We'd like to do this daily if that is all right with you?"

Cecil hesitated. "I had mixed feelings as I watched them. I definitely don't want them ridden into the brushy areas. I'm worried about possible injuries. These are magnificent purebreds."

Donahue could see Cecil wasn't comfortable with his horses' frequent use. "How about we keep it to once a week and out of the thick woods?"

"I'd be more comfortable with that."

"That will be my instruction to the Sergeant. Thank you, sir."

* * *

Gunther and the others had heard the horses snorting and the creak of saddle leather. He sighed when the riders passed them by. "Too close. They came within thirty meters."

"Horses, I didn't even think of that. We're lucky we've not seen any dogs."

After waiting an hour, they crept back to their campsite. After watching with the binoculars for another hour, Gunther concluded the riders hadn't decided to change the security arrangements. They could be back at any time, though. They'd have to be even more alert. He moved their surveillance another twenty meters deeper into the woods to be safe. "We'll have to be more vigilant in watching for the horses so we can catch them early. I hope they don't ride at nighttime. If they do, we need to post a night watch."

* * *

Donahue and Gibbs were reviewing Gibbs's updated security plan when Ballard burst into the office without knocking. Breathless, he said, "Sarge, Captain! You've gotta get to a radio. The Japs are attacking Pearl Harbor!" The two jumped up and followed Ballard back to the troops' day room in the loft. The off-duty guys were bunched around the radio.

The announcer was saying, "*Over three hours ago, forces of the Imperial Japanese Navy, unannounced, attacked America's naval base at Pearl Harbor in the Territory of Hawaii. The attack has been going on for over three hours. This is no joke! This is a real war! Citizens of Honolulu are advised to stay indoors and away from Army and Navy installations! Stay tuned to KGU 760 for on-the-scene updates!*"

Ballard said, "What's it mean, Cap?"

"It means we're at war, son. We'll have to wait to see what impact it has on our mission. Sergeant, stay by the radio with the guys and give me updates every hour. I'll talk with Roberts and our French friends. Maybe with Mr. Cecil, too."

THE WOODS BEHIND BILTMORE HOUSE
DECEMBER 9, 1941

Gunther hardly slept that night. He was concerned about their new surveillance spot. It didn't feel safe anymore. The plan would only work if his team remained undiscovered. They couldn't be seen, alert any sentries, or be noticed by any staff. Any discovery meant a failed mission. Switching the painting only worked if no one had reason to believe its substitute might not be real.

The next morning, he decided to take Krauss and see out how deep the woods behind them were and if any more distant spots still had a line of sight to the southwest windows. Muller was left on the binocular watch.

They cautiously advanced through the woods behind them, roughly a half kilometer. The woods stopped when they reached a large creek. *This must be feeding into the French Broad*, thought Gunther. The creek was wide, maybe ten to fifteen meters. He thought this clear running water would be a much better place to fill our canteens. As he watched, two ducks floated by. *I'd like to fish here.*

Remaining on this side of the creek and turning south, they came upon a grass-lined, deep gully leading west to east. They followed as it wound through the woods and back toward the Biltmore's main gardens. The gardens were reached from the east side of the house via a wide set of marble stairs from the terrace at the southeast end.

He took a knee as the gully emerged into open ground and motioned Krauss down. This was the terrace where the one sentry patrolled every thirty minutes, from the front to the back of the main building. While he was posted at the east side of the terrace, Gunther believed the sentry, while looking to his left, could wave to the picket posted at the north end at the foul weather entry drive-through. Leading straight out from the terrace, he would see the long Biltmore House exit driveway. Glancing to his right, the sentry was looking at the main gardens.

When the south sentry crossed to the southwest side, Gunther figured he saw the Grand Patio to his left and mostly light woods to his right. He could not really see the rear north sentry because of one of two rear abutments in the foundation. Looking straight ahead, he would see the forest. He would see the gully and open ground off to his left. Because of the small clump of fir trees, Gunther could not see the sentry posted behind the carriage house at the northwest end.

Gunther noted that the gully he and Krauss were following was wooded until about the last thirty meters when it emptied into the main gardens.

Motioning to Krauss to crawl to him, he whispered, "I think the sentry can see this gully, but if one of us got closer to that wall of the patio, he couldn't."

"How far do you think it is?"

"About twenty meters."

"I agree. That wall's about five meters high and runs all the way to the garden entrance."

"Let's go back."

Gunther and Krauss scooted to the bottom of the gully and reversed course. Crouching, they walked back another thirty meters, where Gunther climbed up the gully wall on the side leading to their old surveillance post. Lying atop it, seven meters to the right, he looked toward the house. There was the foundation where he'd gone in the other night. Here, he calculated it was about twice the distance from the windows than the old surveillance post. But if he crawled forward another eight meters, he could see the southwest windows. *We're moving here,* he thought.

He motioned to Krauss, and they started back to get Muller and their gear. But Krauss was moving slowly. "You all right, Werner? Has the pain gotten worse?"

"My jaw...really swollen. Hurts, terribly...no complain..."

Gunther was not so sure.

Back at their original surveillance site, he told Muller they were moving again. The three buried their trash, gathered their gear and the little food left, and slowly made their way to a small rise just above the gully. "We'll surveil from here. Every hour, whoever's on the watch will crawl east about fifteen meters and check the windows for the yellow signal." He went on, "We're closer to the creek we found today. We can fill our canteens from there instead of the lagoon where we stashed our boat.

"Werner, I want you to tell me if your pain is beyond what you can bear. I'm serious. Don't try to be a hero."

"Yes, Captain. It is already affecting my sleep. But I'll manage. I hope I don't make noise when I do fall asleep."

"Muller, how's our bread and sausage holding up?"

"I checked it as we moved just now, Captain. We've got maybe enough for two days."

"Well, that's another challenge," said Gunther. "This part of the plan is not turning out so well. Both of you try to get some rest. I'll take the binocs for a while."

Gunther was watching the north end of the complex. There appeared to be more movement than usual. A sergeant had visited both sentries and discussed something. Aside from the mounted patrol, that was the first time he'd seen this.

At this pace, the mission won't make it, thought Gunther. *I'll have to risk the basement again if I don't see the signal tomorrow. We need more food, and badly need something to address Krauss's infection.*

* * *

Donahue thought Antoine Buchard would still be sleeping since he stood watch from 8 p.m. to 8 a.m., but found him already awake. He talked with Phillipe, Maurice, and Roberts in the Living Hall.

"You've heard the news?"

"We have, Captain. We're very sorry this happened to America."

"We'll be at war now. Probably against Japan, Germany, and Italy."

"*Oui*. And Vichy France?"

"Above my paygrade," said Donahue. "I'll call Colonel Powell first thing in the morning. I don't see how this will change our mission here. I'll keep you posted."

"Thank you, Captain. May God smite our enemies. We are all together in this fight now. *Vive L'Amerique!*"

NINE

BILTMORE HOUSE
DECEMBER 9, 1941

Randolph knocked on the office door. "Captain, you have a call."

Donahue wondered who might be calling him. Surely it was official; Alaina wouldn't call him here. Would she? Maybe in an emergency? It was only thirty feet from his office to the kitchen. He stepped out to where the phone hung in the nook.

"Donahue speaking."

"Captain, this is Colonel Powell. The Gallery of Art director, Mr. David Finley, will fly in here tomorrow morning. I believe he's been worried since the Pearl attack. Now that we're at war, everything military-related is a higher priority. I'm bringing him and myself to review your arrangements there."

"Certainly, Colonel. I was going to call you this morning. We'll stand by. Will Mr. Finley be staying over? Shall I set up rooms?"

"Not necessary."

"Yes, sir. Do you foresee any change in our mission here?"

"At this time, I do not."

"Thank you, sir. We'll be ready to receive you and your visitor."

"Captain, I'm sure you're aware of the Sergeant's Grapevine?"

"Indeed, I am, Colonel."

"Well, my Top's telling me you were considering giving your team a day off now and then to go into Asheville to unwind?"

"I guess Gibbs has been on the grapevine," said Donahue, "That's true, Colonel."

"I wanted to help you out with that," said Powell. "I'm going to bring an extra Jeep tomorrow. Your men will need transport."

"That's very thoughtful, Colonel."

"We'll arrive around ten hundred."

"We will be ready, sir. I'll also inform Mr. Roberts his supervisors on his way."

"Good idea."

BILTMORE HOUSE
DECEMBER 10, 1941

The next day, at ten hundred hours, a three-vehicle caravan arrived, with two army Hudson sedans and a Jeep.

Donahue had his men in two ranks at the front of the House, near the covered, foul-weather entry. He'd moved the sentry usually posted there closer to the main entrance so he wouldn't be in the way of the personnel stepping out of their vehicles.

Powell was short and fit, with close-cropped gray hair. Donahue saluted him, and Powell returned the salute.

The Colonel said, "Mr. Cecil, this is David Finley of the National Gallery."

Finley shook John Cecil's hand. "Nice to see you again, John."

"It's been a while, David. Welcome to Biltmore House."

"Mr. Finley, this is Captain Donahue, head of the Army's security team here."

"Good to meet you, Captain."

"Good to see you, Daniel. Miss the Gallery?"

"Excellent to see you, sir. Yes, I do. Would you like to tour our storage area?"

"That's what we're here for. Gentlemen, excuse us. John, I'll get back to you after I review the setup here. Is that all right?"

"Certainly, David." Cecil returned to the house.

After the others left, Donahue said, "Has the declaration of war changed anything for Morris yet?"

"We're to get ready for a massive building program and a huge bump in my TO&E."

"I see. What exactly would you like to see here today, sir?"

"Let's start with the written plan. Then, I'd like to walk around to all the sentry posts."

The Colonel reviewed the written plan in Donahue's office. "This looks good. How about roving patrols?"

"We considered them. Our fixed posts are, in my opinion, effective."

"Let's walk the grounds," said Powell.

They started at the north end of the compound and walked around the rear of the stables, where they checked the northwest sentry post.

The soldier on watch quickly put his cigarette out and snapped to attention, unshouldering his weapon and bringing it to present arms.

"Report!" said Powell.

"Sir! Sentry Post #2, nothing to report, sir!"

"Very well. Carry on, soldier."

They continued around the house, passing the abutment in the foundation and the fir tree-line extending from the forest toward the rear of the house. The pair turned the corner to their left, following the Grand Patio's lower foundation. They briefly entered the lower central gardens, then walked up the triple-wide marble stairs that brought them to the South Sentry post, the south terrace intersection, and the formal driveway in front of the house.

The second soldier, having seen the officers approaching, was standing at parade rest while under arms. As they came close, he came to attention and brought his weapon to present arms.

Powel again barked, "Report!"

"Sir! Sentry Post #3, all clear, sir!"

"Nothing out of the ordinary, soldier?"

"Only the arrival of the Colonel's party, sir!"

"Carry on."

The two officers continued down the front drive. They passed the house's main entrance and approached Sentry #1. The sentry came to attention and presented arms. The officers returned the salute and continued around to the service entrance.

Powell took off his cap and wiped the sweatband with a handkerchief. He ran the handkerchief through his short hair. "What about the outer perimeters?"

"Gibbs and Gatlin rode a couple of the mounts stabled here around the outer perimeters two days ago."

"Really? Before I got my wings, I was a horse soldier. Love to get back in the saddle."

"I'm sure that could be arranged, sir. Mr. Cecil has been very cooperative. But, first, how about a cup of joe?"

In Donahue's office, he took two cups off the end of their table, stepped out to the kitchen area, and filled them. Once back in his office, he told Gibbs to saddle two horses for another perimeter check.

He pulled a chair up. "How are we gonna fight two major fronts, Colonel?"

"The Pentagon has already designated them as the European and Pacific Theatres. I believe the newspapers came up with the phrases. I'd think MacArthur would try to run the Pacific, but the Navy has a good claim of being in charge there. There are two or three top-notch generals who can run Europe. The new draftees and our ability to crank out war production will be our ace-in-the-hole."

"Think we can put men in the field quickly, Colonel?"

"No, we let our peacetime force get too small, and our equipment's outdated. We'll have to shorten basic training, and the first actions those troops see won't be textbook. We'll get some bloody noses." The colonel drained his mug.

"I think you're right, Colonel, but let's hope not. Ready to ride?"

Gibbs had the horses ready. "His name's Vandy, Colonel."

"Thanks, Sergeant."

Gibbs led them out to retrace the ride he'd taken two days before. Powell asked questions as they rode and professionally evaluated the perimeter. They rode to the edge of the forest and halted.

"This is a fine animal," said the Colonel while apprising the woods. "Did you go into this underbrush?"

Gibbs related John Cecil's instructions about the horses.

The Colonel nodded.

* * *

Muller saw them and scooted back to their position. He whispered, *"Ritters,"* and pointed.

Gunther told the other two, "*Scheisse*...let's see if they start into the woods again. If they turn toward us, grab the painting and fall back to the creek."

But the riders remained in the open field. They stopped once by the strand of smaller firs Gunther had used as a shelter before crawling into the bowling alley. They had a long ride skirting the massive main gardens before passing the lagoon and riding down the Biltmore's driveway.

Back at the stables, the Colonel reined up. He was grinning. "What a treat," he said. "A pleasure, Sergeant. First time I've sat a horse since polo at Fort Oglethorpe in '34."

"Any time, Colonel."

Once they'd unsaddled the horses and brushed them down, Gibbs took Powell back to the office.

"How was it?" asked Donahue.

"All right," said Powell. "I'd make only one suggestion. The sentry directly behind the carriage house has a blind spot at the first abutment in the house's foundation. I'd suggest posting an additional sentry where the stand of fir trees comes close to the back of the house. I believe the front two already have an overall view of the front perimeter and a decent field of fire, should it come to that."

"Roger that, Colonel. We'll adjust our security plan accordingly. We could use an additional four troopers to facilitate our rotation if that could be arranged."

"Morris field is flooded with troops. D.C. and Governor Broughton have mobilized the National Guard. Last week, the War Department sent a National Guard transportation battalion of four hundred men. I'll detail an additional four and their equipment. Do you need anything else?"

"More C-Rats, more ammo, a projector, a movie screen, and movies. Gibbs has started a list; it includes some training manuals."

"Gibbs, got your list?"

"Right here, Colonel."

"I'll see what we've got and send it out with the troopers."

Donahue said to Gibbs, "Modify the security plan to include four security posts with six rotations a day. Then, double up another three bedding areas. Tell the men we have movies coming."

* * *

In the third-floor Living Hall, Daniel introduced Director Finley to Phillipe and Maurice. Finley seemed to be immediately drawn to the colorful puzzle crate. Daniel told him the story of the crate and how it had become an extra layer of security for the *Mona Lisa*.

"Fascinating," said Finley. "It's an extraordinary piece. May I see the Mona Lisa?"

"I'm afraid not," Daniel said, "It's part of Captain Donahue's security plan. Only Donahue and Mr. Buchard know the opening sequences. I questioned that, but they politely reminded me the Mona Lisa was France's property. You did see her during our display while she was at the Gallery. I can ask Donahue to open it for you?"

"Don't bother. I did see her at the Gallery. Do you have the inventory sheets you used in the move?"

"Yes, sir. Right here."

After reviewing them, Finley asked if Cecil had acquired any interesting new art for the Biltmore displays.

Daniel said, "I'm not sure what you've previously seen, sir, but there's a room full of interesting Oriental pieces. Mr. Vanderbilt loved Japan. He loved all of Asia. He was very much a world traveler. There is also a Rembrandt in the Oak Sitting Room. The salon has two Monets, and there are two Renoirs in the breakfast room. The library has a ceiling painting entitled The Chariot of Aurora. It's especially nice! The gardens have two original statues, one by Karl Bitter and a 1500's era Italian wellhead. There are half a dozen lesser paintings throughout the house."

"We can see those; then I'll see if Mr. Cecil is available. Did you know our own Manet, the one Mrs. Vanderbilt donated to our museum, is in one of the crates in the third-floor Living Hall? It was on display here at Biltmore from 1890 until the Gallery received it."

"That is ironic. Lead on, Daniel."

After showing the Director around, Daniel went to see if Cecil was available. He was told he was out front with the officers. Finley and Roberts returned to the convoy in the front driveway, where Donahue, Powell, and Cecil were discussing where the war was likely headed.

Cecil said, "Any chance the States could be invaded?"

Powell answered, "Probably not, though the Japs may try a landing in Hawaii. There's too much ocean and too long of a supply line. This applies to both coasts. Also, America is a vast country with an armed populace. Way tougher to gain control over."

After saying their goodbyes and leaving the Jeep behind, the visitors returned to Morris Field.

* * *

Wrapped in their blankets, Gunther and his men peered from their position near the gully. They observed an army sergeant bring a new sentry to the clump of fir trees. They were sure any entry to the maintenance tunnel would be seen from this new sentry's location, and even their old surveillance point might be seen. Entry to Biltmore was now blocked!

He could tell his men were disheartened. Gunther decided to enter the house once again. He needed to address their food needs and Krauss's worsening tooth infection. *But how can I do that now? We are in a pickle. Think, Rolf!*

To keep his men from hanging their heads and feeling dejected, he said, "We'll find another way in. Think only of that. Werner, push aside the pain and run those schematics through your mind again. Conrad, watch to see if any more posts are established. Let me know immediately if the new sentry comes to this side of the fir trees. Think, *kameraden*, think!"

TEN

THE WOODS BEHIND BILTMORE
DECEMBER 18, 1941

Krauss's swollen face suddenly popped up, distorted in a horrible smile. "Yes! There is another entry, and we're now in a better position to use it. A gymnasium equipment delivery door is next to the steps leading to the main gardens. They start at the junction of the south terrace, where it connects to the Grand Patio. A gate then enters a large door. That opens into a corridor that leads to the men's and women's lockers.

"We'd have to enter through the gardens, but now we have this gully to hide us until we get there. We'd be okay there if we waited for the south sentry to walk patrol from the front to the rear. We've watched him do this every half-hour he's on duty. When he's in the back, he can't see the part of the garden we'd be in or the entry grate in the stairway's base. The gardens are at least five meters lower than the road where the north sentry is located. His angle won't let him see us approach the gymnasium gate as long as we stay low."

"Excellent, Werner. I'll try it tonight. We're back in the game."

As the sun declined and the air grew chilly, Gunther started to put together the items he'd be taking: an empty backpack to load foodstuffs, a flashlight, and one of the red lenses. During his last visit, he'd felt the unfiltered flashlight was too bright, which had really worried him outside the staff bedrooms.

At 0030, he crept from their surveillance point down into the gully. Some small animal scurried away, startling him. It smelled like wet gym clothes.

Crouching, he moved down the gully until it began to level out twenty meters from the Grand Patio. Like the house, the Grand Patio's foundation was at least five meters high at the rear. He slowly crawled on his belly across the grass from the end of the gully to the foundation wall. From there, he followed the wall to the edge of the main gardens.

Once in the gardens, he scrambled more quickly through medium to tall evergreens. When he thought he was beyond the view of the sentry, he turned left toward the eight-meter-tall wall separating the gardens from the exit driveway. He crept down this wall for thirty meters until he reached an oversized statue of David, the Jewish shepherd-king. Crouching behind it, he could see the sentry on the south terrace. He waited, heart thumping, until the sentry moved to the rear of the terrace and out of sight. Then, he ran the last ten meters to the gated entryway at the base of the grand stairs, which led from the central gardens to the terrace and the front entrance of Biltmore House.

Opening the gate, Gunther was surprised that nothing here seemed to be locked. He continued on under the terrace for about fifteen meters and came to an ornate medieval-style, oak-planked door. Opening that slowly, he found himself at the southernmost end of the basement level. On his left, as he entered, was a large room. Krauss, from his memory of the schematics, had called it The Halloween Room. There were dim amber night lights built into the baseboards along the corridors. *Vanderbilt's designer might have been a sailor at heart,* thought Gunther. Staying in the corridor, he snaked around to the locker rooms. On the other side was the bowling alley where he had previously entered. Aside from the bowling alley, the entire basement appeared to be tiled. He made no noise as he followed the corridors. He smelled chlorine as he skirted the indoor swimming pool. Keeping to his right in the corridor, he passed the gymnasium lounging room. Shining his flashlight in that direction, he saw nothing of interest. He followed the corridor another six meters as it turned left toward the central kitchen.

Entering the dark kitchen, he used his flashlight to look for any tool that could help him pull Krauss's cracked tooth, but he found nothing he thought would work. He smelled the pastry kitchen before he got to it. Entering, he got a whiff of fresh bread and bananas. He stuffed two loaves and four muffins into his backpack.

Back in the corridor, he turned toward the pantry. There, he jammed four cans of sausages into his bag. The same brand he'd taken before; they were delicious and convenient. He found jars of peanut butter. He'd learned about peanut butter and jelly sandwiches when he and his father had traveled to America to talk business with Henry Ford. It would give the team protein and be easy to eat for Krauss. He loaded two jars, three cans of pork 'n beans, and a large can of peach halves into his backpack. He also got tea bags and salt and pepper shakers. He knew from experience that these would help extract pus from an abscess and stop bleeding when used as a saltwater rinse.

He was about to leave when he noticed a nutcracker set and nuts on one of the shelves. The set had a nutcracker standing upright and a half-dozen nut-picking tools circled around it. They looked like dentist's tools. He pocketed two of the picks.

Turning right out of the pantry, then taking a quick left, he returned to the laundry area where he'd found the blankets on his first foray. Looking around the industrial-looking washing machines, he found a plumber's toolkit. In the kit was a pair of pliers, which he took.

Thinking of the pain Krauss was experiencing, he wondered if there might be aspirin in one of the gym lockers. He turned left out of the laundry and followed the corridor back to the lockers. There was a total of fifteen, including the men's and women's areas. He found a half-full bottle of Bayer aspirin in the fourth in the men's area. Checking the rest of the lockers, he found a shaving kit with a razor and a full pint bottle of Jack Daniels whiskey in the eighth locker. *Here we go*, he thought. As he stuffed the kit in his backpack, he read the word *Germany* on a newspaper lying on the changing bench. Intrigued, he halted.

The headline read, *U.S. At War with Japan and Germany!* Gunther read a second paper's headline. *Japs Attack Pearl Harbor!*

His knees weakened, and he dropped to the bench, breaking out in a cold sweat. Realizing the implications of this development for him and his men, he thought, *we're officially spying now. Every driving movement, waiting on the U-boat, as well as the U-boat approaching the pickup area, will be three times more difficult than it was before the war was declared. Is a painting for that fat Marschall worth this? I don't feel I'm helping our war effort.*

He shoved the newspapers into his pack and got back to his feet. Practically running out of the locker room, he turned right, then right again, traveled another ten meters, and slipped through the ornate door. He checked his watch; he'd been in the basement for an hour and a half. He'd planned to spend up to two; he had to be gone before 0300. That's when the bakers showed up.

Gunther anxiously halted inside the tunnel between the basement entry door and the iron gate to the gardens. At 0305, he calculated that the sentry had probably walked to the rear of the terrace. He slowly descended into the gardens, rushed along the wall on his left, and ducked behind the statue of David. He leaned out and glanced back at the sentry post at the front of the terrace and saw it was empty.

He again followed the wall until turning right into the central garden and following the greenery he had used for concealment on the way in. He left the gardens and quickly hugged the patio's foundation wall. He had to be careful crossing the twenty meters from the foundation wall to the gully. The south sentry was now on the back of the terrace and would have a better view of his path during his crawl into the gully. As he crawled into the gully, the moon was just starting to peek from the cloud cover.

Back at the surveillance point, he told Krauss, "Let's get to it. I'll wash these pliers and the nut picks with whiskey. Drink as much as you think you'll need. We'll use both flashlights with the red lenses; you hold one if you can, and Muller will hold one."

He disinfected the tools while Krauss downed a third of the whiskey. With the two flashlights on Krauss's open mouth, Gunther probed with a pick. Krauss flinched and mumbled "*scheisse.*" After adjusting his entry, Gunther picked up the pliers, seized the cracked tooth, and firmly twisted. The top part of the tooth came off with a crack. Pus began to ooze out. Gunther poked a hole in the side of Krauss's gum where a pocket had formed. More pus spurted out. He took Krauss's flashlight and looked closely.

"Your tooth didn't crack up and down the middle. It cracked at an angle. I can only get the top half out with these tools. This'll help for a while, but with the roots still in place, it'll swell again in two or three days. All I can offer is a saltwater rinse and a tea bag to staunch the bleeding and help draw the pus out. Change it every couple of hours. Take two aspirin every few hours."

"Thanks, Rolf. It feels better already."

"Okay, good. But now, I have bad news." He told them about the headlines. "If we're caught now, we'll be charged as spies and be hung."

He let the information resonate, then added, "I'll let you two decide if you want to continue or abort. Werner and I speak good English. We could likely get by if discovered, if we had no incriminating evidence. But Conrad speaks only a little. He'd be dead. Thoughts?"

The others glanced at one another.

"No other options, Rolf?" mumbled Krauss.

"I see none."

Finally, Muller said, in German, "Double *scheisse*. What the hell? In for a penny, in for a pound, Captain, for the Fatherland and der Fuhrer!"

Krauss took another swig of whiskey, then nodded in agreement.

"Back to it, then. Werner, it's cold, but try to get some rest. Keep up the rinse and the tea bags when you're awake. Conrad, get some sleep. Eat some of the sausages if you're hungry. That might help you relax. I'll get some shut-eye after daybreak."

* * *

Donahue had decided to keep the plan for Christmas leave. The puzzle crate and a single Frenchman on watch would keep the paintings safe while the other two Frenchmen were on leave. He didn't see how the declaration of war would affect their mission. If anything, he felt that the coming war would create less incentive for thieves to be concerned about stealing art. The two Frenchmen had left this morning and were due back on the 26th.

* * *

At midnight, on the first night of watch by himself, Buchard found himself developing second thoughts. Regardless of the consequences to himself or his family, he couldn't let the Germans steal France's national treasure.

But maybe he could make the best use of the Louvre's donated copy, which they always carried as a backup. Of course! The Germans surely couldn't have anyone traveling with this team who could distinguish a Chaudron from the real thing.

Having decided, he retrieved the copy from his room and returned with it to the Living Hall. Unknown to Donahue, Buchard had seen the captain prick the edge of the museum's *Mona Lisa*. With the two paintings propped side-by-side in front of him, Buchard now duplicated the pinprick on the Chaudron and switched the two. He couldn't be sure Donahue wouldn't want to inspect the painting again. He placed the Chaudron in the crate, then wrapped and returned the World's Fair *Mona Lisa* to his room.

It was time to place the signal. He pinned a bright yellow ribbon from the sewing room to the back of the curtain in the South Tower Room.

The rest of his watch was as uneventful as usual. Buchard spent it reading about the conservation of old paintings. *Maybe I should write a book,* he thought. *I understand everyone has at least one book in them.*

* * *

Too cold to sleep, Gunther was watching the house. At 0100, a light came on in the South Tower. That had never happened before.

"There it is," he said, lowering the bird glasses. "A yellow ribbon. Exactly as instructed."

He told Krauss to watch here, and he and Muller would go in. Buchard would be the sole guard in the artwork room. Reichsmarschall Goring had forwarded the instructions just as Gunther had requested.

At 0200, he and Muller crawled down the gully, over to the foundation of the raised patio, and into the main garden.

At the statue of David, they halted to make sure the south sentry was already on the backside of the terrace. They eased open the iron grate. It creaked loudly. They quickly stepped through and shut the gate.

Standing motionless, they could hear the sentry's boots scuffing across the terrace. Gunther could actually see the sentry's arm as he whistled toward the front north sentry and motioned as if to check for any movement. The north sentry must have replied because Gunther could hear his boots returning to the rear of the terrace.

Waiting another five minutes, they slowly opened the ornate door to the basement level. They followed the corridor through the locker rooms and onto the bowling alley. Once there, Gunther used the red light to find the door to the stairs leading to the third-floor entry into the South Tower.

* * *

At 0200, Buchard almost jumped out of his chair as Daniel Roberts pushed aside one of the curtains and entered the Living Hall.

The National Gallery's curator stood looking at the puzzle crate.

"Daniel?" said Buchard.

"I can't sleep. The craftsmanship of this thing is all I can think of. I had to come in here and admire it again."

He spent fifteen minutes poking and pressing on the exterior of the crate. He finally quit and walked over to Buchard. "I've tried to open this thing at least two dozen times. Did you find it hard to do, even with instructions?"

"Yes. It's ingenious."

Buchard's palms were sweating. The Germans could appear at this very moment, and he had no way to signal them to hold off until Roberts left. Would they be carrying guns? Would they kill everyone? Did they know about the soldiers outside? Did they just arrive at Biltmore? How did they get past the guards and up the stairs?

* * *

Exiting the South Tower Room, Gunther heard voices. He held up his hand for Muller to halt. They stood listening. Gunther wondered if one of the talkers would leave through the curtain directly in front of him. Motioning Muller to step back into the South Tower Room, he did the same. He could barely hear them from there.

* * *

Roberts chatted for another ten minutes, mostly about well-known collections, then said, "I can probably sleep now. Thanks for listening." He stepped back through the curtain.

* * *

Gunther heard the conversation end. After another moment, he stepped out of the room and up to the curtain. He heard nothing.

They waited another five minutes before pushing aside the curtain and tip-toeing into the Living Hall.

Gunther, cocking a baseball bat, along with Muller, entered, and Buchard stood.

"Antoine Buchard?" said Gunther, while Muller, awestruck, just stared at the man.

"Yes. What, exactly, are you here for?"

Gunther lowered the bat.

"The da Vinci. What else? Where is it?"

The Frenchman pointed to the crate.

"What the hell is this?" said Gunther, wanting to grab the *verdammt* painting and get out of there. He pushed on the crate. It didn't budge a millimeter.

The Germans took a closer look. Muller said, "That's a piece of art in its own right. Are you saying the Mona Lisa is in there?"

"It is," said Buchard. "Do you think you can open it?"

Still miffed at the unexpected obstacle, Gunther said, "Normally, I'd love the challenge. But I do not have the luxury of time. Open it, or you and your family are done."

Reluctantly, Buchard went through the sixty-four steps. This took twenty minutes, and Gunther was getting visibly edgy.

As Buchard opened the final compartment, Muller swung off his backpack and carefully fished out the team's copy.

Pulling the painting from Donahue's crate, Buchard reluctantly handed it over to Muller, who handed Buchard the Goring painting in return.

"Reichsmarschall Goring purchased this after WWI," Muller said. "I attended your lecture at Heidelberg University in 1934. When you spoke about old-master preservation. I truly enjoyed that. I'm sorry we're meeting under these circumstances."

Buchard shrugged, "Fate will punish you barbarians."

Muller held the painting at arm's-length. "She is lovely. Is this the real thing?"

"What do you think? We hang fakes in the Louvre?"

Muller continued to view the front and back of the painting, spending five minutes doing this. Gunther, restless, glanced at his watch and peeked out the entrance curtains, noting the room's many rows of crates.

While that was going on, Buchard glanced at the German copy. *I must admit, this is a masterpiece of a copy.* It was difficult to distinguish the two, even side by side. *I'll compare it against the real thing on my next watch.*

"Will there be anything else?" he said stiffly, "Or have you enough loot for now?"

"There will not," said Gunther. "I will contact those holding your grandparents. I'm sorry we met under these circumstances."

"Thank you, but just leave," said Buchard, feeling ill, as if he'd handed over his own child to the Nazis, even though he'd given them a copy. Just chatting with them made him feel like a traitor.

* * *

Gunther helped Muller sling the special backpack, and then they crept out. Gunther stepped into Vanderbilt's bathroom in the South Tower Room and picked up a bar of soap.

After descending the hidden staircase and following the corridor back, they exited through the ornate door near the Halloween Room. They stopped at the iron gate. Listening for the sentry, Gunther hissed, "Wait here."

He rubbed the soap on both sides of the hinges. He prayed the door would not squeak again. It did not. Leaving the gate open, he slowly entered the garden.

A thick fog had rolled in. He could barely see three meters. Returning for Muller, he led the way back through the garden, around the patio foundation, then out into the gully, and back to where they'd left Krauss.

They found him asleep amid their backpacks and other gear. Gunther shook him. He looked up. "How'd it go, Captain?"

"You were asleep!"

"I'm sorry, sir. I must have passed out. The pain's worse again, even with the whiskey and aspirin. I finished the bottle."

"It's all right, Werner. We're leaving. Bring the blankets; we'll hide them in the park when we return the boat."

After burying their trash and loading their packs, they walked through the fog back to the Lagoon. They found the skiff still hidden. Uncovering it, they loaded everything and started rowing down the French Broad.

The going was tough. The heavy fog made them nearly run into the bank at three different points. They almost missed the park where they'd left the Ford. Luckily, at the last moment, Muller, taking a chance and pulsing his flashlight, spotted a reflective *Hires Root Beer* sign on the rental shack.

Tying up, they took their gear, including the special backpack and blankets, and walked to their car. The blankets and backpacks went behind the rear seat, and they loaded the painting in the back seat with Krauss.

Gunther decided it was too foggy. "We'll wait for this to lift. Try to get some rest. Werner, try another salt rinse. We have two tea bags left."

Krauss mumbled, "*Alles Fur Deutschland, Herr Kapitan.*"

"No more German," Muller reminded him. "Or else keep quiet, Werner!"

Eventually, the fog lifted enough that Gunther decided to chance it, at least to get out of the immediate vicinity.

This time, he'd have to drive. He'd reviewed his maps while the others were trying to rest. After a false turn, he finally found the highway to South Carolina. "We have about eight hundred kilometers to drive. We'll need gas up sometime in the next one hundred kilometers. I'll try to find a grocery with a pump out front. I'll see what else I can buy to help your tooth, Werner."

But Krauss was slumped with his eyes closed. He didn't answer. Pus drooled from the corner of his swollen mouth.

COLUMBIA, SOUTH CAROLINA
DECEMBER 22, 1941

Outside Spartanburg, they filled up and checked the oil and tires. Gunther bought a bottle of aspirin and poked around in Krauss's mouth to release more pus. In the one hundred and fifty kilometers since Columbia, Krauss had become almost delirious. Gunther doubted he'd be able to make it to the coast. He discussed it with Muller. "He has the best chance of passing for an American. We've got to either drop him here or get rid of him."

"Do you mean…"

"That's one option. I'd rather not do that."

"Me neither."

"Okay, hospital it is. The aspirin has worked to calm him a bit. He's no longer delirious, but he's lethargic. We'll leave him with enough money to lie low until he can escape to Mexico or somewhere else to get out of the country." Doing otherwise would jeopardize the entire mission and possibly Krauss's life.

"We're sorry, my friend, but this moment of less pain is not going to last. Do you understand, Werner? I've placed some money in your pocket."

"It must be done."

Using the last tea bag, they made Krauss a drink. He sluggishly nodded his understanding. They dropped a barely functioning Krauss at an emergency room entrance. Muller took over the backpack, and they headed for the coast.

* * *

After the emergency room doctor had given Krauss a shot and drained more pus from the infected tooth, he gave him some pain pills and said, "That'll be five dollars, please. I see from the check-in log you're Jonathon Turner. Are you from Columbia, Mr. Turner?"

"No, sir," slowly replied a partially recovered Krauss.

"Passing through?"

Recovering more each moment, Turner, sticking with his cover story, said, "I'm a Chapel Hill student. After the damn yellow Japs bombed us, I wanted to join the service. I was on the way to the recruiting office."

"Well, this is your lucky day. Sergeant Summers from Army Recruiting is in the next room. We're fixing his broken finger. Did you drive here?"

"No, I had a friend drop me off on his way home for the holidays."

"All right! A rush of young men joined up after the sneaky attack on Hawaii. Summers can take you in with him, and you can jump the line. If you pass the physical, you'll be in the Army in four hours. They'll pull that tooth for you, too. Heck, a college student? They might even make you an officer. Good luck, and give the Krauts and the Japs hell from us folks back home."

Krauss pondered his situation. He understood why the team had to leave him. He didn't feel in danger; he'd spent four years in this area, and he knew he could blend in. His current choices weren't difficult to understand. One, stay with his cover story and be inducted into the U.S. Army, or second, make some excuse to allow him to escape out a back door and later be caught as a spy.

Army, here I come, thought Krauss. *This will give me time to rest and plan. I can disappear after basic training, and I'll have better identification papers then.*

SURFSIDE BEACH, SOUTH CAROLINA
FAMILY CAMP GROUNDS
DECEMBER 22, 1941

Gunther and Muller lay in the tall grass along the dune line all night. It was cold, the waves were choppy, and the sand was blowing heavily their way. Worse, he saw a Coast Guard cutter patrolling on the far horizon.

"They must have added this patrol after December 7," Muller whispered, "We're screwed here, Captain. When's the boat due back? I forgot."

Gunther was worried. U-127 had orders to return for three nights starting December 22nd. "If they don't see us, they'll head back."

"What if they've sunk her?"

"We have two more nights before we'll worry about that."

Gunther wasn't sure where the two of them would spend their day while waiting for nightfall. They could sleep in the Ford during the day if they could find a secluded spot, but more than one night might rouse suspicions.

U-127
OFF SOUTH CAROLINA
DECEMBER 22, 1941

At 0200, Kapitan Bauer ordered U-127 to ascend to periscope depth.

"Up scope," commanded Bauer. He performed a quick 360-degree sweep with the periscope. "Surface contact bearing 290°. Down scope!"

"Contact appears to be an Active-Class Coast Guard vessel. The Active-Class was recently upgraded to include depth-charge racks. They are now classified as submarine chasers. We won't be approaching the beach today. Helmsman! Right full rudder! Come to course 110°. Ahead slow. We need to conserve batteries."

"Right, full rudder, come to course 110°, ahead slow, aye, Kapitan," replied the helmsman.

"XO, assume the conn," said Bauer.

"I have the conn," replied the executive officer.

U-127 moved away.

SURFSIDE BEACH, SOUTH CAROLINA
DECEMBER 23, 1941

The sea was less choppy on the second night, but the cutter was still on the horizon. Two civilians with a shotgun and a rifle were patrolling the beach. The two Germans were growing despondent.

"What are we going to do, Rolf?"

"Maybe Mexico. Cuba's too far, even if we could steal a motorboat. We've still got tomorrow night." They still had access to the Ford, but gasoline was now likely rationed.

"Let's see if we can remain undetected through today."

* * *

At the beginning of the third evening, the cutter was still out there, steaming in a zigzag pattern, and the civilians were still patrolling. Shotgun had widened his patrol area and was coming within fifty meters of their position.

Gunther was ready to give up and leave. But at 0100, the cutter pulled out of its pattern and gradually headed south. Seeing the cutter move off, the shotgun-toter and the second civilian headed into town.

Gunther and Muller felt their spirit's lift. After another half hour of no activity, Gunther started blinking his flashlight toward where he believed the U-boat might be. Ten minutes later, he received a return signal. He almost jumped up and shouted.

Through the bird binoculars, he watched the crew launch a large dinghy. It would have been faster if they could have rowed their old dinghy out, but it was slashed and stored in another town. The crew made slow progress in the choppy water. Gunther continued to blink every few minutes to guide them in.

The dinghy reached the beach, and the two Germans climbed aboard with their backpacks and the painting. Slogging through frigid water, but with the wind behind them now, the dinghy returned to the U-boat faster than it had taken to reach shore.

U-127, Gunther, Muller, and the Mona Lisa slowly departed from the shoreline.

It was Christmas Day in America. In Germany, in the new year of 1942, Goring and Hitler would be having a late Christmas party, with the Louvre's backup *Mona Lisa* as their honored guest.

BILTMORE
DECEMBER 25, 1941

After an excellent Christmas dinner hosted by Mr. Cecil, Buchard, Roberts, and Donahue enjoyed a glass of tawny port and the finest of Cuban cigars in the Gentlemen's Room.

Buchard wished everyone a Merry Christmas, thanked Cecil, and excused himself to take a dinner plate to Jules.

Phillipe and Maurice would return from leave tomorrow, and the watch sections would revert to their old schedule. He'd decided to tell Roberts he was no longer needed in the rotation since they had two for each shift, though he could still do the 8 a.m. to 4 p.m. schedule if he wanted to.

After midnight, he decided to thoroughly compare the Louvre's World's Fair *Mona Lisa* against Goring's Chaudron, which the Germans had switched for the Louvre's backup copy. Buchard could now account for the Louvre's original and two Chaudron copies. He had the museum's *Mona Lisa* and the German's Chaudron copy. The Germans had the Louvre's donated Chaudron copy. This was getting confusing. He might have to jot down some notes.

He made a quick trip to his room to get the Louvre's *Mona Lisa*.

Propping the two paintings side-by-side on two crates and removing a lampshade so he could get more light, he started comparing the German copy against the Louvre's. Buchard initially ignored the frames. When the painting was returned in 1914, the Louvre had reunited it with the frame Vincenzo Peruggia had discarded in the Louvre's hallway when he'd stolen it in 1911.

Instead, he compared the size, the general aging, da Vinci's unique paint application, and stroke techniques, including the 'smokiness' others had noted in da Vinci's works. Along with the other details, he'd usually check to identify fakes. Now, he noticed slight differences in the amount of glazing and the darkness. The German copy had a substantial amount of additional glazing. The small cracks in the paint, called craquelure, were also more pronounced on the copy.

He checked the figure's hands, where the glazing was known to be thinner. Once again, the German copy appeared more correct than the Louvre's painting. Buchard's heart raced as an idea began to take hold.

He thoroughly inspected the back of both paintings, searching for the repairs he knew had been done to control the warping. The two "dovetail" recesses, the bottom one walnut and the top one with its canvas-filled insert, and an additional canvas strip pasted over a small crack in the panel. Early restorers had applied these repairs; later, a second fix had placed the canvas in the top dovetail recess. The repairs were present in both paintings but appeared older and more professionally done in the copy the Germans had left.

This fit the known history of the repairs undertaken over the decades to arrest the warping of the poplar panel.

Buchard continued checking. The H and the number 29 written on the back of the painting were present, and both appeared to have the correct conte crayon and pencil attributes. The hand-written *Jaconde* on the upper left and the other recorded markings on the rear were all present. But these features looked older in the German copy.

Buchard was dumb-struck. He flopped back in his chair. Could the theories that had cropped up after the return of the painting in 1914, that the one returned to the Louvre was not the original but a masterful copy, be true?

When a concerned collector donated a copy attributed to Chaudron to the Louvre in 1928, Buchard and others thoroughly inspected the two. Buchard had only been at the Louvre for a year then. They'd detected hardly any differences.

Could that have been because they were both Chaudron copies? Had they inspected a Chaudron against a Chaudron?

That possibility was bewildering, even terrifying, but exciting! Could the Germans have ended up with the *original* when Goring purchased it? With the seller and Goring both believing it to be one of the six copies?

Had they now forced him to exchange it for what everyone thought was the original? Was the real da Vinci finally in the hands of the French for the first time since the 1911 theft?

Buchard now believed that was exactly what he was holding in his hands. "*Vive la France!*" he muttered. The lovely La Jaconde was back!

* * *

In case Donahue wanted another surprise inspection, Buchard duplicated the captain's pin prick on what he now felt was Leonardo's *Mona Lisa*. He also switched frames between the old *Mona Lisa*, which he now suspected to be another Chaudron copy, and the authentic, German-switched *Mona Lisa*.

The Louvre had always been in possession of the frame, making that, at least, undeniably authentic. Buchard gently placed the genuine work inside the puzzle crate. He stored the old Louvre version, which had been thought to be the veritable one, in an unused crate. He would take it to his room later. He'd run more tests, but he felt sure that what was now in the crate was the real da Vinci.

* * *

Buchard now had a dilemma. Would he dare share this story with anyone else? Doing so would reveal his complicity in the theft and the switching of the paintings.

In the end, he decided to let history continue to believe the *Mona Lisa* had always been in France's possession since her return in 1914.

He lifted the glass of port he'd brought to the room, "Merry Christmas, France," he said aloud. "Here's toasting the loveliest woman in the world!"

BOOK II:
PERUGGIA'S STING

ELEVEN

(FOUR MONTHS EARLIER)

THE SENATE OFFICE BUILDING
WASHINGTON DC
AUGUST 8, 1941, 2:00 PM

Roberts checked in at the desk in the Senate Office Building. "Good afternoon. I'm from the National Gallery of Art. Senator Wellington's expecting me. Mr. Trace Raines asked me to stop by. He's —"

"The Senator's aide. Yes, sir." The receptionist checked her calendar. "I'll buzz his office."

Raines was smartly dressed in a bowtie but looked like a college student on the way to pick up a date. They walked across the first floor of the Russell Senate building. The statue of Senator Russell stood far away across the marble floor. The rotunda featured a round balcony showing two floors of office rooms. The beautiful dome, far above, was built of dark Tennessee marble. They took the elevator to the basement and rode a motorized cart to the Senator's office at the other end of the massive building.

Raines remained in the outer office. Roberts looked around, nodding in approval. The room housed two button-tufted dark leather armchairs, a medium-sized Louis XV writing desk, and mahogany paneling with a half-dozen vintage artworks. He recognized works by Van

Gogh, one of his thirty-five self-portraits, and *Bathers*, by Cezanne. Large Tiffany gold and glass lighting sconces separated each painting. Fine art lamps were mounted above each masterpiece. *Lord in Heaven*, he thought, *Millions of dollars, just on these walls.*

Wellington came in looking energized and outgoing. He had a full head of wavy gray hair, a neatly trimmed black and gray mustache, a tailor-made dark blue suit with a blue striped shirt and French cuffs, a pocket square, and a dark bow tie. Combined with his piercing dark brown eyes, he presented an imposing figure that instantly bespoke power and wealth.

Shaking hands, he said, "Daniel, good of you to pop over." He pointed to a plush sofa. "Shall we sit?"

Lighting a cigar, Wellington said, "I asked you here to discuss your upcoming trip to North Carolina with the artwork from the Gallery. I was a member of the committee that chose the Biltmore as a haven for the nation's treasures."

"Yes, sir. We're almost ready to move the selected pieces."

"When are you leaving?"

"The day after tomorrow."

The Senator paused as if thinking. "Can you come to my house for dinner tomorrow evening, Dan? If I may call you Dan?"

Daniel's expression must have shown surprise. He finally said, "Well, yes, Senator, I can."

"Fine, said the Senator. I live at 1313 NW N Street in Georgetown. Let's say, seven pm?"

"Thanks for inviting me, Senator."

GEORGETOWN
AUGUST 9, 1941, 7:00 PM

Pulling up in front of a stately row house, Daniel found a parking spot on the tree-shaded street. It looked like rain; he rolled up the windows on his old Chevrolet coupe. He jogged up the steps and rang the doorbell. While he waited, his hand went into his left pocket as he fidgeted with his lucky nickel. The doorbell chimes played "Hail to the Chief." *Pretty presumptuous*, he thought. But Wellington isn't far behind FDR in appealing to his party's faithful. He might be tapped for VP in '44. It could happen.

Too bad Carol divorced me. She'd have eaten this up.

A maid opened the door. She took him to the study and told him the Senator would be right in.

The Senator sauntered in. He was wearing a maroon-colored velvet smoking jacket and slippers. "Welcome, Dan!"

"Pleased to be here, Senator. I love this room. The whole house, actually."

"Thanks. I own the place next door, as well. My father bought it in 1910, and I purchased it in 1930. I rent the one next door to a fellow senator. A Republican, but not a bad fellow…this way to the dining room. I'm afraid Mrs. Wellington is back home. One of our grandchildren has a recital. I hope you like quail."

The meal consisted of oven-roasted quail served with pasta and a bottle of Merlot from Beaulieu vineyards in California. Wellington held the bottle up for Daniel to read. "They have a new winemaker named Tchelistcheff from France. He's doing wonders in changing their processes and increasing sales. I tried to buy in, but it's privately owned."

After they finished their meal, the cook served an outstanding Baked Alaska for dessert.

"This was marvelous," said Daniel. "I can honestly say this is not my usual evening meal."
"Shall we go back to the study? I currently have a Renoir, two Rembrandts, and a lesser Jan van Eyck, which I think you'll enjoy."
After carefully viewing the paintings, Daniel said, "These are very nice, Senator. I could easily see one of the Rembrandts hanging in the Gallery."
He laughingly said, "Thanks, but I'll keep it here. But that's very kind, coming from someone with your background. A scotch?"
"Yes, please."
"Ice or no ice?"
"One cube, please."
He poured two generous glasses of The Balvenie 21-year-old single malt. "Please, be seated." Wellington lit another expensive-looking cigar. "Cigar or cigarette?"
"Thanks, only occasionally smoke a pipe, Senator. And I'm trying to give that up."
As they sat and admired the paintings, the Senator said, "Mind if we get serious?"
"I thought we were being serious, Senator?"
"This is…personal serious, Dan. I'm sorry to hear about your divorce. As for your other troubles, I'm told the Boo-Boo Hoff mob is holding your marker for $5,000."
Displaying his poker face, Daniel took his time sipping his scotch. "However would you know something like that?"
"Oh, I have contacts all over, Dan. I'm not judging you. I want to help you keep all your limbs intact. The Hoff mob doesn't play as nice as Jimmy, the 'Gentleman Gambler' who previously ran the Maryland Athletic Club.

Now, if you'd like to be immediately debt-free and rich soon after, I might have a proposition for you."

Daniel cleared his throat. What could the man want in return? "You have my attention, Senator."

"Would you like to see my very private collection?"

"Where would that be, sir?"

Wellington turned and pressed a hidden button under his desk. A remote panel on the far wall slid open, and fine-art lamps illuminated ten paintings on the walls of the revealed room. Daniel guessed it to be about 8 feet by 10 feet.

The two men stepped in.

He stared like a deer caught in headlights. *The Just Judges* by Jan Van Eyck and *Portrait of a Young Man* by Raphael hung on the walls. He was almost sure he was seeing something by Caravaggio, though it was obviously Caravaggesque. There were others he didn't immediately recognize.

They all appeared to be pieces that he and the rest of the art world thought had been stolen and were gone forever.

Catching his breath again, he saw da Vinci's *Mona Lisa!*

Wellington checked out his reaction. "Isn't she a beaut? I'm sure you've heard the story. This is one of the six copies by Yves Chaudron, painted in 1912. When Peruggia stole the *Mona Lisa*, Chaudron had access to her. He planned to sell his fakes to rich Europeans and Americans, each believing they had the original. He even developed advanced aging techniques during his two years of painting his copies.

"I came upon this in 1917 as an army supply officer in Paris. A St.-Cyr officer's father had died in the Battle of the Somme. The son didn't care about it and offered it to me. I didn't have much cash, but he and I made a deal for tires, oil, and other goods I had in our supply depot. We were both pleased."

Daniel studied the copy closely. "It's astonishing! Even though I've studied the original many times, this is almost indistinguishable."

"Here's what I need of you, Danny-boy," said Wellington. "I need you to switch this one for the real deal when you get to the Biltmore. I'm willing to pay you two million dollars. And that ain't hay! By switching, not stealing, the painting, no one'll be looking for you or her afterward. If you agree, your debt to the Hoff mob will be paid off tomorrow, and there'll be a nice chunk of change left over."

Daniel flopped down in the only chair in the small room. *Two million*, he thought. *I could move to California, either Los Angeles or San Francisco, and open my own gallery.*

"May I see the reverse?"

"Of course."

Roberts reviewed the other side of the poplar panel. "It's well done but questionable in the area of the dovetail stabilizers. I think what you want can be done if I can spend some alone time with the original. I'm assuming she'll be crated. I'd need at least an hour. I'll need an advance to bribe a few people. When would I get the two million?"

"Excellent, Dan. Let's say an advance of $5000. Call Trace tomorrow and give him your bank. I'll take care of your gambling marker. Let's say, $100,000 to your account tomorrow. The bribe can come out of that. The rest when she's delivered?"

"Let's say the bribe money's extra," said Daniel.

"Really? Fine, I won't quibble, but don't push your luck! Trace will call you tomorrow. Shall we celebrate with another scotch?" He sauntered back into his study.

Daniel left the row house with the carefully bundled copy.

THE NATIONAL GALLERY OF ART
WASHINGTON, DC
AUGUST 10, 1941

The following day, he packed the Chaudron and some clothes in a trunk and, after loading them into his car, drove downtown to the Gallery. He planned to follow the moving vans and the French guards to Asheville.

The museum personnel were carefully loading the modified moving vans. Daniel decided to wait in his office. He walked across the dark marble floors into an area off-limits to the public. Behind the personnel offices was the large storage area for works not currently being displayed, as well as maintenance and restoration studios.

Daniel shared an office with head Curator R.J. Rogers and another Assistant Curator, Eugene Autry Jenkins. The curators' office was at least fifty feet by fifty-five feet and had ten-foot ceilings. It was cluttered—with art posters displayed around the upper walls, empty frames stacked against one wall, a desk in each of three corners of the room, a large center table with mockups of planned displays, and four large bookshelves filled with reference volumes.

One of Remington's twenty-two bronze sculptures, *Mountain Man*, sat on top of a stack of books, and a small ivory carved statue was being deployed as a doorstop.

R.J. Rogers was away from his desk.

Daniel said, "Gene, I'll be in North Carolina for who knows how long. I'm leaving now. Any calls for me should be forwarded to R. J."

Displaying his usual lop-sided grin, Jenkins said, "Don't forget your lucky nickel." He then went back to reading a reference book on Fredrick Sackrider Remington.

Before he left, Daniel retrieved three books from the shelves to take with him. He would have lots of free time at the Biltmore Estate, and there would likely be no poker games.

On his way back outside, he reminded the receptionist, "I'll be in North Carolina for the undetermined future. Mr. Rogers should be contacted for any business calls to me."

"Yes, sir, Mr. Roberts."

The trucks were ready to leave. Daniel waved at Antoine Buchard and then the drivers. As the trucks rolled off, he fell behind them, and the Frenchmen followed him.

BILTMORE
AUGUST 11, 1941

They arrived at the Estate the next afternoon. Daniel had been here in the early 1930s when it had first opened to the public. He didn't know the Cecils personally, but his supervisor, Rogers, knew Cornelia Vanderbilt Cecil and her deceased mother, Edith Vanderbilt. Daniel had heard from Ray Rogers that Cecil's marriage was strained. Rogers had phoned them and smoothed the way for Daniel's arrival.

* * *

The caravan was met by the Cecils in the large front driveway. Daniel introduced himself, Buchard, and the assistant curator, Phillipe. The two policemen stayed with the van drivers.

Mrs. Cecil said, "Please use any rooms you deem necessary. If you need us, just ask Randolph, our head man."

Daniel thanked her, then joked, "I expected to arrive with tour buses all around."

Mrs. Cecil said, "When the relocation committee asked to use Biltmore, they also asked if we'd suspend the tours for a while. Senator Wellington even insisted the government pay us the average monthly income we'd received from last year's tours."

"I'm glad Senator Wellington is involved," said Daniel. "He's a strong supporter of the arts. Just not so much when it comes to American artists."

Before Daniel continued schmoozing with the Cecils, he asked Buchard if he would go through the house to identify the best places to store the paintings and suggest sleeping arrangements for the five of them.

As the others talked, Buchard excused himself.

TWELVE

ATLANTIC OCEAN
DECEMBER 26, 1941

Gunther, Muller and Bauer sat crammed together in U-127's minuscule wardroom.
No one had asked about Krauss or Hellwig's absence. The crew probably thought Muller was Hellwig. However, Gunther had introduced Muller as Lieutenant Muller to Bauer, and the captain said he could hot-bunk with the engineering officer.

"I'm glad your mission was successful, Captain. Though I know you can't discuss it."

"Thank you, Kapitan. You were a big part of our success. I'll be reporting that to the Reichsmarschall."

Bauer looked worried. "But we're in a bit of a situation, Gunther. The extra two days waiting to pick you up while we dealt with that cutter has left us lower on fuel than I like. We're almost out of diesel. We can run on the surface on batteries, but that would slow us down and our range is limited. It would add days to our traveling to a milk cow. Just as important is the fact we're almost out of food. We have about a week's rations left, and it will take a little less than two weeks to get to the replenishment rendezvous.

We've already been on half-rations for days. We can't move the milk cow close toward us because she has to stay outside the range of land-based aircraft. Since December seventh, Yankee patrols have doubled."

"We'll try to stay out of your way, Kapitan. Muller and I have a few sausages left from our last store stop; they'll last us a few days. I'm sorry for the extra time it took to get off the beach."

"Not your fault. In war, plans change every half-hour. You two might want to get some rest now."

Gunther slept in the same rack he had used coming over. Muller had to wait until the Engineering Officer got up to go on watch. The special backpack was lashed to the bulkhead where Gunther slept.

On the way to his bunk, Gunther and Muller passed the chief petty officer Gunther had once seen washing with alcohol. "Chief, we've been in these clothes for weeks. We must smell like wet sea lions. Can you find some cologne and rags?"

"Certainly, Captain. I'll have one of my men bring them to you. We also have a machinist who was a barber in Munich."

"Very good, Chief."

ASHEVILLE
DECEMBER 28, 1941

At the table in the main library, Daniel dug through the card catalog. After fifteen minutes of searching, he found only three reference numbers he thought might be promising.

Having given up on breaking the sequence of the puzzle crate on his own, he'd decided to research puzzle boxes. This might give him more insight into the tricks employed over the ages when building them.

Pulling out the two books he could find, he browsed them. One showed a few illustrations of how to open Oriental puzzle boxes, but they were straightforward: 3-step, 7-step, or 11-step boxes. He needed something showing more examples and more complex opening sequences.

At the librarian's desk, he asked about the reference number he couldn't find. The librarian explained that the library was on a lending program with the University of North Carolina. Another library had requested that particular volume. If he wanted, she would call the university's library and request they send up to five books that fit any category Daniel would like to research. "Those normally arrive within two days."

"That would be wonderful. Can you request any illustrated book that references Oriental puzzle boxes? I'll return in two days."

The librarian said she would order them.

ASHEVILLE PUBLIC LIBRARY
DECEMBER 30, 1941

When he returned, he found three volumes waiting. The first two were better examples than those he'd found in the local branch. The third was a treasure. It was three hundred and fifty pages long, with hundreds of drawings of opening sequences and tricks used by box makers. It did have one drawback. The book was printed in Chinese.

"Are you kidding me," he muttered.

The book could not be checked out, so he spent three hours browsing, taking notes, and copying the drawings. He was intrigued by 'incline steps', which involve tilting the boxes. *That won't be happening,* he thought. Some designs actually included blueprints.

BILTMORE
JANUARY 1, 1942

In the third-floor Living Hall, Roberts wished the Frenchmen on watch a Happy New Year. He added casually, "I thought I'd start '42 off by trying to crack this damn puzzle one more time."

Phillipe said, "Good luck, Mr. Roberts," and returned to reading.

Daniel's spirits rose when he opened sixteen of the opening sequences within forty minutes. He found two more sequences in the next hour but was stymied again after two hours. Giving up, he closed the steps he'd opened. Moping on the stool he usually used for his watch duties, he pulled out his lucky nickel and started twirling it. What could he try next?

Phillipe, the assistant curator, noticed his twiddling. "Is there some story about the coin you so often play with, monsieur Roberts?"

"Well…there is. While I was a college student, my roommates talked me into going to Atlantic City, New Jersey, for a night out. I didn't have much money; I barely could afford college. But I scraped two dollars in nickels together to use at the slot machines.

"When we got to the casino, I chose a machine close to the bar, and the very first time I put a nickel in and pulled the handle, I hit a two-dollar jackpot. As the payout of nickels fell into the belly of the machine, one nickel jumped over the lip and fell on the floor. I reached down to pick it up and noticed it looked different.

"It turned out to be a 1916 double-strike-date buffalo head nickel. I'm not a collector, but I had heard others say double-strike coins could be valuable. I put it in my left pocket so I wouldn't accidentally spend it. To this day, it's been my lucky nickel."

"That's a good story," said Phillipe, smiling. He turned and repeated the story in French to Maurice, on watch with him. Maurice also smiled and nodded.

On the way out, Daniel said, "As you probably noticed, I had some success on the crate. But the results were the same in the end: another flop. I'll have to say, good job to the carpenter. A beautiful and very clever piece."

In his room, he studied his notes from the library. Given the book's language barrier, he'd tried all the tricks he could. The crate was just too complicated for him to open by himself. He could only access the painting inside if Buchard or Donahue opened it for him.

How could I get one of them to do that, he wondered. As far as having something in their background that might be used against them, Daniel's gut told him Buchard was a more likely candidate than the Army officer.

He decided he'd search Buchard's room while Antoine was on watch that night. He might learn more about him and find something he could use to coerce him into helping. Two million was enough to split if that was what it took.

At two o'clock in the morning, he slid into the Hoppner Room at the rear of the third floor. His own room was up the hall and opposite Buchard's.

He took a chance by opening a closet door and turning on a light. That gave him enough illumination to search without showing too much light under the door. He did have to be quiet since the Walnut Room had a connecting door to the Hoppner.

He found nothing of interest in the dresser or under the mattress, nothing in the bathroom, and nothing hanging in or on the closet shelf. At the foot of the bed sat a mid-sized steamer trunk, much like the one Daniel had brought to the Biltmore.

He opened the trunk and pushed aside a raincoat. Under it was a painting. He took it out and carried it to the light.

It was a *Mona Lisa!* And a very nice one indeed. He quickly decided it had to be another of the Chaudron copies. But what was Buchard doing with it in his room?

He set the painting back in the trunk, just as he'd found it. Then, went back to his room to think through this find.

If the Louvre legitimately owned Buchard's copy, why wasn't it on the inventory of items moved — and in a crate in the Living Hall? He could possibly use this against Buchard. But, if it were legit, it would reveal Daniel's having broken into Buchard's room. *Too many ifs,* he thought.

Wanting to smoke his pipe but ignoring that desire, he leaned back and visualized having Buchard under his thumb.

Daniel summarized his dilemma: He could not open the puzzle crate. He was determined to get the two million dollars Wellington offered. He had this amazing find. He had to use it somehow. A plan began to form. He would swap Wellington's Chaudron for the copy in Buchard's room!

His plan would ensure any markings Wellington might have made on his copy would not be present when he returned this new copy to the Senator. Daniel would also switch the frame from Buchard's copy with the frame from Wellington's. This was for two reasons: Buchard might notice the frame was different from what he'd been looking at for who knew how long. And Wellington might have marked his frame. Buchard's frame would continue to be what he was used to, but Daniel would have to do something about the frame from Wellington's copy. He certainly could not use it on Wellington's new copy of the *Mona Lisa*.

After checking his watch, he crept back to Buchard's room with Wellington's copy. He had removed the frame. He switched the frame from Buchard's copy to Wellington's. He placed the Wellington, with Buchard's frame, back in the trunk just as he'd found it.

Back in his room, he temporarily put Wellington's frame on Buchard's copy and hid it in his own trunk until he could find an off-site storage place. It was too much of a risk to keep it here.

Shaking from excitement, he could no longer resist the urge. He opened his drawer and pulled out his pipe and his Prince Albert tin. Loading and lighting, he puffed away. This calmed him as he pondered his next steps. What about the frame?

THIRTEEN

MID-ATLANTIC OCEAN
JANUARY 4, 1942

U-127 pulled alongside the large Type XIV submarine. The latter was new, the first 'Milch Cow' tender in the German Navy.

Gunther noticed the XIV had a fatter hull than U-127. Also, she had no gun. "No deck guns?"

"And no torpedo tubes," said Bauer. "The gun was eliminated to facilitate the portable cranes used in the refueling and resupplying. But she does carry torpedoes to resupply attack boats. The sea's not that rough here. In the North Atlantic, her decks would likely be awash, and the resupply would have to come up through the conning tower, adding twice the time."

"These mother ships will contribute mightily to the efforts of our attack boats, allowing us to stay deployed for long-range missions. Our older boats can go 11,000 km, and our newer boats 15,000. Germany needs more bases for her U-boats. Without these, we will have to return to France or Germany for refueling and resupply and run a dangerous anti-submarine gauntlet there and back."

Bauer and Gunther watched the operation from the conning tower of U-127. Bauer said, "This is her first mission. She is the first of ten planned in the Atlantic. Without them, we wouldn't have operations in the southern Atlantic and Indian Ocean." Refueling and passing aboard food, spare parts, and an additional torpedo took three hours, and then U-127 was again on her way. While taking aboard supplies, the U-boat's cook immediately started a fresh meal for the crew. Sailors in the working party reached into the fruit crates and ate what they could grab as the crates passed.

After another thirteen days, they pulled into the pens at La Rochelle.

The war against Russia had started with amazing successes but was increasingly bogged down in tough fighting and a brutal winter. The war effort hampered every other German need for goods, transportation, and other war materials. Non-Russian Front-related transport aircraft and even train schedules had all but come to a standstill. Even a call to Reichsmarschall Goring's office couldn't expedite transportation. Gunther and Muller could not get a flight to Berlin until early March.

FORT JACKSON, SOUTH CAROLINA
U.S. ARMY INFANTRY BASIC TRAINING
CLASS 41-53
JANUARY 12, 1942

Private Turner had just completed his second week in the Army. At times, it felt good to have no concerns about where to go and what to do. His drill sergeant did all the scheduling for him and his fellow recruits. Turner remembered his Luftwaffe training officer had told him and his fellow cadets, "Ours is not to reason why; ours is but to do or die." He believed it came from the poem

"The Charge of the Light Brigade". That saying appeared to apply to all military duties, even basic training.

Sergeant Summers, the recruiter, had given Krauss, now 'Jonathon Turner,' a ride to the recruiting station. The two had talked on the way, and the recruiter said he was encouraged that Jonathon had completed three years at Chapel Hill. He said Jonathon would be sent to Officer Candidate School when his transcript came in.

Of course, the Army would never receive a transcript under that name.

He thought he'd decide later when and where to bid farewell. Meanwhile, the rest of his tooth had been extracted. He felt good, even rested. His drill instructor seemed pleased with his bearing and adaptability. He'd been made a squad leader. He and the others had been informed that basic infantry training usually lasted thirteen weeks but might be shortened due to war needs.

In the chow hall, he'd overheard two DIs saying the Army was planning to land troops in Africa soon. They also said the first wave would likely be parachute-trained infantry.

After another week of basic, the men were tested to see if they would qualify for continued training. Turner, who had already been classified as an outstanding recruit, asked for parachute training.

After graduating, he received orders to continue to Fort Benning, Georgia, for seven weeks of parachutist training.

* * *

The Army gave them three days off after basic training. Jonathon spent his time reading every newspaper he could find, researching the war in Europe. *North Africa is as close as I can get to German units,* he thought. *I could be home within a few months. I wonder if Rolf and Conrad made it back?*

FOURTEEN

HOLLYWOOD, CALIFORNIA
JANUARY 12, 1942

Dear Sister,

Happy New Year! Thank you for changing my life. I was in a rut for years until you nudged me into making decisions. As usual, I hope this finds you and Clifford doing well. I haven't been here a month, but I feel much healthier.

I found a small apartment one block off Sunset Boulevard. It's quaint and worlds away from the 250 rooms at Biltmore. I've even been to the beach! A bus stop is a half-block from my front door, so I can go anywhere I desire.

I have a job interview tomorrow. I might be working for a young actress named Barbara Stanwyck. Wouldn't that be grand?

I'm sorry you can't return to Germany anytime soon. I do hope you get to live the life you're envisioning.

My address is:

Elise Schneider
6609 Leland Way

Hollywood, California

Please stay in touch.

Much love, your sister,
Elise.

JAGEMANN'S GALLERY
JANUARY 18, 1942

Dear Elise,

    I'm glad things are going well for you. Clifford and I are separated at the moment. In late November, I told him I was selling the gallery and wanted a divorce. At the time, that news didn't seem to shake him. With the consulates closed in all the U.S. cities and the embassy mothballed in Washington, no visas are being issued for travel, and since that traitor Roosevelt declared war against Japan, Germany, and Italy, who would want to go to a place the rest of the world hates?
    The art trade has come to a standstill since war was declared. I doubt I can keep the gallery open much longer. I will use the money from our joint transaction until it runs out. Then, I can sell a couple of my own paintings at fire sale prices. That should get me by for another six months. I'll be out of cash if the war lasts over eighteen months.
    Having some of Clifford's money to get through this would have been nice, but I've burned that bridge!
    Enough of my problems. I'll get by. I always do.
    Have a wonderful life out in Hollywood!

All my love,
Lillian.

FIFTEEN

BILTMORE
JANUARY 19, 1942

Donahue received another call from Colonel Powell in his office on a newly installed telephone line.

"Donahue, here."

"Good morning, Captain. We've got another visitor wanting to come to Biltmore. Senator Archibald Wellington. He doesn't want anyone to know it's him until he arrives. Anything I can bring?"

"First off, we'll be ready, Colonel. Secondly, it's been unseasonably cold here. Could you have your Supply Officer issue us thirteen cold winter parkas? We'll need six-large, five-extra-large, and two-2X-large. Gibbs and I already have tanker jackets, and I secured gloves and thick socks from a local store."

"Call the S-4, Captain. Tell him you talked to me. See you tomorrow."

* * *

When the Senator's car arrived, Mr. Cecil, Roberts, and Donahue were there to greet him.

After Colonel Powell introduced Donahue, Cecil, the Senator, and Roberts headed inside.

They felt they didn't need to follow, so Donahue, Powell, and Gibbs headed for the stable's courtyard.

The Colonel said, "My S-4 says the coats will be here tomorrow. How about another ride around the perimeter?"

Donahue said, "Yes, sir, certainly. I'll see you when you return."

He stepped into the carpenter's shop to greet Joseph.

* * *

Gibbs said, "Colonel, it's quite cold, but the horses should be okay."

"We can turn back if it's too harsh."

In the stables, they saddled the same mounts they'd ridden previously. Trotting out the door, they entered the area behind the house, and Powell returned the salute of the shivering sentry.

"I see you installed sentry post weather covers. It's funny how such a small change can make a mind-numbing duty more bearable."

"Captain Donahue and I try to keep the men happy, sir. This duty can get boring."

They rode on for another sixty yards, past the recently added sentry post #2. It had the same overhead shelter for the sentry to stand under. Powell again returned a salute. He said, "Let's head into those trees a little way and see how deep the forest goes."

Gibbs said, "Mr. Cecil has concerns with us riding his horses through rough terrain."

"We'll be careful," said Powell. "I'll thank John for letting me ride."

After dodging scrub bushes for seventy-five yards, they found a wide creek. Following the creek leftward, they found a gully that led back toward the house. The Colonel eased Vandy down into it, and Gibbs followed. After sixty yards, the gully debouched at the end of the South Terrace and the Grand Patio.

The Colonel stopped and looked left, then right. He swung down and stood next to his horse. "Look how this depression covers me to my neck. If I stooped and walked through it, the post on the South Terrace wouldn't see me. The Grand Patio cuts off his view."

Gibbs jumped down and shaded his eyes. "Absolutely right, Colonel."

"I'd suggest either moving the recently added sentry to this side of the clump of fir trees or adding a second on the Grand Patio. If he stayed on the rear side of the Grand Patio, he could see the entire gully until it merged into the woods. In addition, the #3 sentry would not have to patrol from front to back like he's doing now."

"True, Colonel, but we're stretched as it is to man the rotation schedule we now have with fourteen personnel."

"With the influx of Guard troops at Morris, I can send you four more. That would staff a new four-hour rotation."

"That would work, Colonel. All I need to do is find bed space."

"How about they bring four bunk beds with them? That'd keep the number of rooms down."

"That'd be great, Colonel."

They returned the horses, unsaddled them, and brushed them again.

Powell patted his mount lovingly, "A refreshing ride, Sergeant."

"The pleasure's all mine, Colonel."

* * *

An hour later, Cecil, Wellington, Powell, Roberts, and Donahue were enjoying a roast beef and cheese tray lunch in the informal dining hall.

"I understand the War Department is considering rationing gasoline," said Cecil.

"They are," Wellington said. "I think that will happen soon. Also, other categories. All rubber goods, all canned foods, even shoes. The other day, one of the staffers suggested rationing bicycles because of the metal and rubber required to manufacture them. It'll be uncomfortable, but I believe the American people will get behind rationing."

"Where do you think Hitler will strike next?" Cecil asked, looking at Powell.

But Wellington spoke up again. "The War Department believes Hitler made a major mistake attacking Russia. German forces are now facing a really bad Russian winter and will be tied up for months, if not years."

They talked about what generals and admirals Roosevelt might promote as the Army and Navy rapidly expanded.

Finally, Wellington said, "John, on behalf of the American people, I'd like to thank you again for helping to secure many of our treasured artworks."

"I could do nothing less, Archie."

As everyone rose, Powell, Donahue and Roberts also thanked Cecil for the lunch.

* * *

After lunch, Roberts, Wellington, Donahue, and Powell made their way to the Living Hall to view the art. As Wellington came in, he was drawn to the crate. He walked around it. "What an astounding piece of woodwork!"

He kicked it lightly. It didn't move. "Heavy sucker, too!"

"That's our added security for the Mona Lisa," said Donahue.

Phillipe, the assistant curator, said, "Mr. Roberts has spent many hours here testing it." He grinned at Daniel.

Wellington walked through the rest of the Living Hall, looking at the crates of priceless artworks. "Is this all the eighty-two pieces?"

"It is," said Roberts.

"I see an easel. Have you had some on display?"

"We had the Mona Lisa out to do the test fitting for the custom crate," said Phillipe.

"I'd certainly like to see her," said the Senator. "If that wouldn't be inconvenient, that is."

"I'm sorry, we can't do that, sir," said Donahue.

"What? And why not?" Wellington sounded astonished as if he'd always had every whim immediately addressed.

"It's part of our security agreement with the French, sir."

"Poppycock! Remember, I'm why these paintings got here, gentlemen." He huffed, turned, and left.

Daniel sighed. "I'd better go smooth his feathers."

Powell chuckled. "I'll get my folks ready to leave. Thanks for the hospitality, Captain. I hope the cold-weather gear helps."

* * *

Away from everyone else, Wellington asked Daniel, "What progress?"

"I've tried to open that crate eleven times. I've gone to the library to learn more about building and opening puzzle boxes, and I've ordered one more book on that subject. The one I've ordered is about boxes with twenty-one steps or more. I believe that will help me crack it."

"I hope so. If not soon, I want my Chaudron and all my money back. And you can deal with your debts yourself. Understand?"

"I do, Senator."

The senator went to say goodbye and again thank Cecil for his hospitality. Then, he went outside to where the Army vehicles were parked. He found Colonel Powell and Captain Donahue wrapping up.

Since Wellington had upped the heat, Roberts went to the Living Hall to have another shot at cracking the box.

* * *

Donahue was telling the Colonel, "Sir, I'd like to request one more thing. My men didn't have a chance to see their families at Christmas. Five are married. Would it be possible to provide temporary relief so I can give them leave?"

"We can work that out, Captain. When?"

"Starting next Monday, sir?"

"I'll make that happen."

The visiting party piled into the car and returned to Morris Field.

DOWNTOWN ASHEVILLE
JANUARY 20, 1942

The next day, Daniel drove his old Chevy into town. That morning's newspaper had an advertisement for rental apartments above Dot's All-You-Can-Eat Restaurant and Billiard Parlor. This might be a safe spot to move the Chaudron copy. It was offsite from the Biltmore but easily accessible.

Speaking to Dot herself, he rented the room for twenty dollars a month. The place was small, featuring only a single bed, a chest of drawers, an end table, and a small closet. The bath was three doors down. He could reach it from a door next to the restaurant entrance or from the rear. Dot insisted Daniel take a tour. She mentioned a poker game or two could usually be found in the back room of the billiard parlor. Daniel told her he'd check that out. The old itch was still there, and it had been a while since he'd played. His skills needed honing. Daniel had noticed the soldiers playing poker in the loft over the carriage house. Perhaps he could get some practice there?

Returning to his car to retrieve the painting, he placed the wrapped Louvre Chaudron in the closet, then drove back to the Estate. He needed a detailed plan for Wellington's painting.

BILTMORE
MARCH 9, 1942

In his room toying with his lucky nickel, Roberts kept going over what to present to Wellington. The more he thought about his plan to scam the senator, the more he felt it was right. It was what he deserved, and no one got hurt but Wellington. He now felt some relief about his part in the heist. As an art professional, he'd felt dirty about agreeing.

He started a mental list of tasks to accomplish his plan for the new copy. He needed a frame other than the one Wellington's copy used. While on a prior trip to San Francisco with his then-wife, Daniel had heard about a master carver who'd duplicated the Renaissance-era frame on the *Mona Lisa* since 1909. He ran a woodcarving workshop in Sausalito, the artistic hamlet just across the Golden Gate Bridge.

Daniel and his ex-wife had been in San Francisco because he'd heard of an art gallery there that had acquired an estate when a well-known California collector had passed away. He'd wanted to purchase a piece for one of his well-heeled friends in Washington. He'd heard of this master carver's workshop, where a student's final project was to duplicate the *Mona Lisa's* current frame.

Finding more information on the woodcarving school should be easy. When things settled down at Biltmore, he'd contact the carver to purchase a frame or two. He would ask the carver to help him find a suitable finisher who could appropriately antique one or more of the student's final project frames.

BERLIN
MARCH 11, 1942

Gunther and Muller finally flew to Berlin.

Goring was not in town when they arrived, so they placed the *Mona Lisa* in Gunther's office and posted an Air Ministry guard at the door. They spent that evening contacting family and friends to tell them they'd returned.

The next afternoon, Goring sent Sergeant Reicher to bring Gunther and Muller to his office.

They brought in their package and carefully unwrapped it. Finding no easel, Muller propped the painting on one of the couches.

Goring bent to study it closely. "What a wonderful thing," he said. "I'm pleased. I believe more promotions are in order. Captain, you are now Major Gunther. Lieutenant, you are now Captain Muller. By the way, where is Krauss?"

Gunther told the story of the tooth infection and the increasing inability to function. "I believe he was captured or possibly executed, General."

"That's regrettable, Rolf. Let's promote him posthumously, and perhaps an Iron Cross? I'll have my gray mouse do the paperwork on the promotions and Krauss's decorations. She'll set up a meeting with der Fuhrer to officially present this unbelievable acquisition!"

NORTHEAST OF BERLIN
MARCH 26, 1942

Hitler had agreed to meet at Reichsmarschall Goring's country home, Carinhall, named after Goring's late wife.

Gunther, Goring, and Muller entered Goring's Mercedes-Benz 540K Cabriolet-C in front of the Air Ministry. They left the city limits, and the country scenery became quite beautiful for this time of the year. Gunther thought *You could momentarily forget a war is going on*. After traveling the autobahn for eighty-five kilometers, the driver turned onto a wide dirt road. After another few kilometers, they passed a guard house and turned in through two large mountain-stone columns. The driveway was at least a kilometer long. Twenty-five meters before pulling up to the large Swedish-style lodge, two giant bronze statues stood: an Amazonian warrior riding a magnificent horse and a 15-point Royal stag.

Inside, they were met by a fifteen-meter-long entry hall with valuable artwork on both walls. Muller's mouth dropped open, and he halted.

The two officers ate dinner with Goring and spent the night. The next morning, Hitler and his staff arrived. Goring met him in the front driveway, and the officer's arms shot out in the Party greeting. The group entered Goring's oversized den, where Gunther and Muller held the *Mona Lisa*.

Goring stood grinning like a proud student, while Hitler stood with hands on his hips, taking in the painting.

Watching him, Gunther, who had never met the Fuhrer, was surprised at how courteous the Boss was to those around him. *Here's a man who can have millions killed at the nod of his head, and he's acting like a first-year art student.* He seemed to have a habit of twitching his index finger under his nose as if he were tickling his mustache.

Finally, Hitler said, "You've outdone yourself, Hermann."

"I'd hoped *mien Fuhrer* would be pleased," gushed Goring.

"It will be the centerpiece of my Fuhrermuseum. Too bad I can't put the French railway car from our 1918 dehumanizing capitulation next to it," said Hitler.

"Will my Fuhrer join us for lunch?"

"I'm afraid not this time, Hermann. I have a meeting with my generals to discuss strategy for our next Russian move. We've slowed down. I'll have to fire another general," said Hitler, "but thank you for this excellent gift."

He turned to Gunther. "Major, thank you and your team for retrieving this magnificent piece. I give you one more task. Personally deliver this to Hans Posse at the Fuhrerbau Building in Munich. We've not officially started on the Fuhrermuseum yet, though Speer has drafted the plans and had a model made."

"Right away, *mein Fuhrer*."

"Make sure it's featured in the next acquisitions album you present," Hitler said to Goring.

"Yes, *mein Fuhrer*."

Goring, Gunther, and Muller walked Hitler and his party to the waiting vehicles.

Entering his Mercedes, Hitler said, "You can't top this, Hermann. The art world belongs to Germany now."

* * *

"Come inside, and we'll have a schnapps," said Goring, looking both pleased and relieved, as if he was very happy Hitler had left.

Once seated in the study, he said, "Do the two of you have a preference for where you'd like to be stationed next?"

"I'd like Plans and Ops," said Gunther.

"I'd like to be attached to Admiral Canaris's Abwehr if he'll have me," said Muller.

"No problem. You'll be taken care of by my staff, Rolf. I'll speak to Canaris on your behalf, Muller, assuming he's not still at odds with me. It should help.

"Before you take the Mona Lisa, let me give you some background on the Fuhrermuseum. Der Fuhrer has been planning a German National Gallery of Art since the mid-1920s.

"It was originally designed to be in Berlin, but Berlin already has four major museums. He then decided to make Linz, his hometown, the cultural center of the New

Reich. Der Fuhrer's private preference is for the early Germanic artists. Still, his chosen director of the proposed Fuhrermuseum, Dr. Hans Posse, has convinced Hitler a truly world-class museum should include the Old Masters and other works."

"That's an amazing plan," said Muller. "I'd love to work there after we've won the war."

"Since construction has not started, the substantial number of pieces already collected are stored in three separate buildings, one in Munich, one in France, and one in Linz. I'd expect you'll find Posse here in Berlin, but he could be in Munich. I'll have Reicher call and check for you. I'll also have the driver take you wherever Posse is located."

"Jawohl, Herr Reichsmarschall," said Gunther, clicking his heels and bowing. But eager, above all, to be out of there, away from Goring's self-importance.

FUHRERMUSEUM STORAGE FACILITY
THE FUHRERBAU BUILDING, MUNICH
MARCH 28, 1942

The Reichsmarschall's driver left Berlin early the next morning and took Gunther and Muller to Munich. The drive took almost five hours. Thanks to Reicher's phone call, Posse was expecting them.

As they walked through the storage area, the first artwork Muller pointed out was the *Madonna of Bruges* statue by Michaelangelo. "This is the only work by Michaelangelo located outside of Italy during his lifetime. Napoleon took it in 1794. It was returned to Italy twenty years later."

Continuing to the main hall, the next piece Muller pointed out was *The Astronomer* by Johann Vermeer. "I can't believe this," said Muller. "This, like the Mona Lisa, is one of the world's most renowned paintings."

Posse met them, and Gunther had Muller unwrap the *Mona Lisa* for him.

"Truly the world's most amazing creation," said Posse. "It will be the centerpiece of the Fuhrermuseum. Can I show you around? Most items are in crates, but we keep a few on display for when the Fuhrer might want to drop by."

Although Gunther knew Muller would love to look around, he declined. "Thank you, but we have new duty stations to report to, and it's a long drive."

They shook hands with Posse and climbed back into Goring's Mercedes. Gunther instructed the driver to take them back to the Air Ministry.

Arriving at five in the afternoon, Gunther and Muller went to their office to collect their belongings. They then went upstairs and checked out with Reicher before they left to report to their new assignments.

In front of the Air Ministry, they shook hands. Gunther said, "Thank you, Werner, for your work on this mission. I hope we don't lose contact with each other. I'm not sure how long this war will last or where we'll wind up. Good luck with your new duties."

"And good luck to you with yours, Rolf. I'm glad you got me out of the camp. We'll have an amazing story to tell our children someday. I'll try to keep in touch."

Muller headed for Abwehr headquarters, and Gunther went back into the Air Ministry to report to Plans and Operations.

CALIFORNIA
MAY 27, 1942

Phoning the gallery he'd visited in San Francisco, Roberts found that Stanley Holt still ran the carving workshop. The final project for his students was to create a replica of the 1909 frame from the Louvre's *Mona Lisa*. Holt had sketched the frame when he visited the Louvre in 1921 and made his masterpiece in 1922. The students had to replicate his carving.

Upon their graduation, he kept his students' final carvings, displaying the best examples in his shop in Sausalito.

During his previous visit to San Francisco, Daniel had wondered aloud to Holt who, in the U.S., had the skills to distress one of these final frames to match what the Louvre owned. Holt had told of just such a refinisher who'd come to Sausalito to speak. The refinisher had experimented with ways to distress modern-day frames to appear old-world for collectors of portraits from the sixteenth and seventeenth centuries. He'd been experimenting for ten years and had developed authentic-looking techniques.

From Dot's, Daniel called the carving master long-distance and asked if he could purchase two of the students' frames. He said he was going to try to get the National Gallery to display this aspect of art collecting. The teacher said he'd sell him two of his choice.

Daniel tried to make arrangements to fly to San Francisco. But, because transportation was limited to the war effort, he was unsuccessful. Calling Wellington's office, he asked the aide, "Trace, this is Daniel Roberts. I'm in Asheville. I need help with the Senator's special project. I need to fly to San Francisco and back as soon as possible."

"Good morning, Daniel. Let me see what I can do. Give me a number to call you back."

Trace called that afternoon and said tickets from Asheville to San Francisco would be at the American Airlines counter tomorrow at 9:00 a.m.

Once in San Francisco, Roberts took a taxi across the bay to Sausalito. Holt met him and showed him his 1922 work. Daniel was amazed at the exactness of the frame when compared to the photos he'd taken in the National Gallery just last year.

"This is fantastic. I'd pay a pretty penny to buy it."

"I've had offers, but I must display it for my students to copy. I'm flattered you're interested."

Holt showed him a selection of his students' work. Daniel picked the two best, and Holt charged him $200 each.

"Say, do you have a phone number for the refinisher we talked about?"

"Let me look in my office."

Ten minutes later, he returned with the address and phone number.

"His name is Bobby Sledge, and he lives in High Point, North Carolina. He said his entire family has been in furniture building for over thirty years."

"Thanks, Stan. I'll let you know if the Gallery display is approved."

Daniel flew back to Asheville.

He stayed at his apartment that night. The next morning, he drove the three-hour trip to High Point. Once there, he introduced himself to Sledge.

"I've just returned from visiting Stanley Holt in San Francisco. The National Gallery would like to do a display of the Mona Lisa's different frame usage over the centuries. I'd love to showcase Holt's carving work and your own masterful techniques on distressing woodwork."

"National Gallery, huh? Sounds interesting," Sledge said, clearly intrigued.

"It should appeal to our patrons. To do that, I'd like both frames refinished to match my color photographs from the National Gallery display. The first I'll use in the Gallery's display; the second, I'll keep for my own pleasure."

Daniel thought it would make an excellent display piece or could even be offered for sale in the Sausalito gallery he'd decided to open after he left Washington.

Sledge looked at the detailed Kodacolor photographs Daniel had taken of the framed *Mona Lisa* using his Bantam Special camera at the Gallery the prior year.

"I'd like to try it," said Sledge. "A sixteenth-century version would be my greatest challenge so far."

"Wonderful," said Daniel. "I'm on assignment right now, so I'm hard to reach by telephone. I'll call you in two months. Is that okay?"

"I might need three, but you can check my progress in two months."

"Excellent. Can you estimate how much this job would cost?"

"Since it's for the National Gallery, minimal," said Sledge. "Say five hundred?"

"Would you like an advance?"

"That would be appreciated."

"I have a hundred dollars on me."

"That'll do."

Daniel handed it over, shook Sledge's hand, then drove back to Asheville.

* * *

Since Buchard slept during the day, Daniel checked in with him and Donahue once the Frenchman was up and in the eating area. He told them his extra assignment had taken him to San Francisco. The Gallery was designing a new display, and he was responsible for picking the subject matter and gathering the pieces.

"What's the subject?" asked Buchard.

"You'll appreciate this, Antoine. A landscape study showcasing Monet and his mentor Eugene Bouldin."

"I know their works, Daniel. Excellent choices."

Apparently, the routine had stayed the same in the four days Daniel had been away. He spoke to the Frenchmen on watch duty in the Living Hall, then spent a few hours relieving Phillipe from his watch duties.

* * *

Two months later, Daniel called Sledge and was told he could pick up the frames in three more weeks. Daniel had no idea how long it would normally take to distress a piece of wood so it would be accepted as having been made in the sixteenth century, but three months seemed to be fast work.

SIXTEEN

COLUMBUS, GEORGIA
MAY 27, 1942

Turner graduated first in his class from the Parachutist School at Fort Benning and was advanced to corporal. One week later, the Second Battalion of the 511th Parachute Infantry Regiment sailed for Scotland to train with British paratroops. This was in preparation for Operation Torch, the upcoming invasion of North Africa. The 511th then flew from Scotland to Cornwall. The following week, they flew from Cornwall, 1500 miles, over Spain and on to Oran, Algeria, to assist the British forces in their battle against the Vichy French and the troops of General Erwin Rommel.

Turner had planned to desert, return to Germany, and resume his real identity. But, after hearing the drill sergeants' conversation in the mess hall at Fort Jackson, he'd decided to wait his time and not go AWOL in the U.S. *From what I've seen so far, we don't have much to worry about from the U.S. Army. We have much better training, equipment, and experience. But these troops sure do have a bone to pick with the Japanese.*

He would make his break once he was in Africa.

BOBBY SLEDGE'S WOODSHOP
HIGH POINT, NORTH CAROLINA
JULY 3, 1942

Daniel had driven the 160 miles from Asheville to High Point in three and a half hours. His last trip had taken three hours, but he ran into construction on Highway 64.

The two frames awaited him atop a workbench. Sledge had presented the front of one and the reverse of the other. The gold leaf was dark and flat. They were well-aged and looked very used. Both included the minor imperfections Holt had copied while sketching the frame at the Louvre in the 1920s.

"So, Mr. Sledge, step me through what you had to do to replicate the frames."

"I used a layer of American Walnut stain to match the exposed wood tone on the 1909 frame photos you left with me. Then, I used twenty-three karat gold leaf and aged and distressed the frame using steel wool and a burnisher to scrape and wear away the leaf to match the condition in the photos.

"I spent as much time on the back as I did on the front. It required much more distressing. There are many long hours of work here."

"It shows. They're magnificent. Masterpieces, really," said Daniel. "How much do we owe for these wonderful pieces?"

"Would $500 be too much?"

"For this work? Not at all."

He paid Sledge the balance, wrapped the frames carefully, and headed back to Asheville.

ASHEVILLE
JULY 5, 1942

Roberts stored both the custom frames and Buchard's Cauldron in his rented apartment above Dot's. He noticed the frames did have a vague chemical smell. Sledge had told him this could last for up to four months. It was caused by resins and solvents continuing to seep out. He left the frames uncovered and placed them on the bed to air. He decided to research to see if this process might be hurried along.

He pulled out his handkerchief from his left pocket to wipe the frames down one last time; as he did so, unseen to him, his lucky nickel fell out of the handkerchief and rolled under the edge of one of the frames.

I'll check back weekly to see if these still have a smell to them.

BILTMORE
AUGUST 11, 1942

Daniel had been searching his car and the Biltmore House for a week. He couldn't find his special nickel. He hoped he'd not lost it at Sledge's workshop. While searching near the kitchen service entrance, he overheard one of Captain Donahue's men.

"Sarge, I just got back from town. I was in the restaurant eating dinner with a gal I picked up at the movies. We were all rushed outside because the apartments on the upper floors caught on fire. So, I took her to a bar for a couple of drinks."

"Did you get lucky?"

"Nah, she said the fire had her concerned. She knew somebody who lived there. She left to check on them. So, I just came back here."

Roberts' skin crawled, and his hands grew clammy. The hair on the back of his neck felt alive. He reached out to a door frame to steady himself. Going back to the third floor, he made up a story that he had a girlfriend who lived next to the fire at Dot's. He told Buchard he had to run in and check on her.

* * *

He found the front of the building blackened and dripping with water from the firehoses. Smoke still steamed upward, and the smell was like strong, damp charcoal. The scene was noisy, with shouting firemen and clanking equipment. He went around the block. The apartments in the rear appeared to be intact, but the owner and a fireman would not let him or anyone else in. The damp, smoky smell was less intense on this side.

He had to wait two more hours before the residents were allowed up to check on their belongings.

In his apartment, he found everything damp and smelling of smoke. He checked on his *Mona Lisa*. She was dry but had a heavy smell, like right after one doused a campfire. The custom frames also smelled. He'd left them unwrapped so the paint could continue to cure, so they were also damp.

Making sure no one was around his car; he took the painting downstairs and locked it in his trunk. He'd wrapped a dry blanket from the apartment around the wrapping already on the painting.

Back upstairs, he wrapped a dry sheet around each custom frame. Under one, he found his lucky nickel.

Grinning, he told it "You did it, boy." One at a time, he carried the frames to his car.

He planned to return in a couple of days after Dot had cleaned up. He'd work on getting the smells out of the painting and frames. One such trick used at the Gallery was to lightly spray sheets of paper with white vinegar, crumple the sheets, place them and the painting in an airtight wrapping, and leave for a week. Then check to see if the process needed to be repeated.

"Hey, you!" yelled a fireman as he was closing the trunk. "No one can stay here tonight. The fire investigation's going on. Dots got y'all rooms at the Shady Pines if you need somewhere else to stay?"

"Thanks, don't need a room."

He heard Dot also say the nightly poker game was suspended until further notice. He felt good that this news did not distress him in any way.

It's a good thing the soldier was here and came back to tell someone about this, he thought. *If I'd not shown up, Dot or the firemen might have checked the rest of the apartments for damage and discovered the painting. The whole plan could have gone haywire. Actually, I'd have been without Wellington's copy, and he'd likely have had Leo from the Hoff gang take care of me.*

It had been close to disaster, but his lucky nickel had pulled him through.

SEVENTEEN

ENGLAND
SEPTEMBER 8, 1942

Ten C-47 Dakotas took off from St. Eval airfield in Cornwall. Each carried twenty-two paratroopers. They would drop over Tafraoui airfield in Oran, Algeria, to secure the airfield from the Vichy French fighting on the German side.

It was night and three pilots got separated and were hopelessly lost. They dropped their paratroopers many miles from Oran. Turner's plane dropped its stick far to the northeast, closer to El Eulma. As he descended, Turner could make out dark shapes of mountains to their north and open desert to the south. When they regrouped on the ground, they dug in for the night. The lieutenant told them they'd head west first thing in the morning to link up with the others. He estimated they'd been dropped over fifty miles beyond their intended zone and were approximately five miles west of El Eulma.

Turner remembered from their operation briefing before taking off that the last known German battle line was to the northeast near Ouenza.

That night, he slipped away from his unit. After hiking four miles east, he entered a small village. He believed he was just outside El Eulma. The street stank of goat dung. A few flat-roofed, mud-brick houses were scattered about, and a wellhead sat in the center of the village. Only three vehicles could be seen. He decided to ditch his carbine, along with everything except his army undershirt, trousers, and boots. From here on, the less he looked like a U.S. soldier, the better.

In the center of the village, he found a French-made Renault Monaquatre sedan. Thanks to his father's owning a dealership, he knew how to hot-wire a vehicle. Before attempting it, he pushed the Renault a little way from the owner's home. After getting it started, he drove out of the village. He hoped his German language and the French vehicle could get him past any Vichy troops he might encounter.

Twenty-five miles northeast of El Eulma, he fell asleep at the wheel, and the Renault rolled off the road into the sand and stalled out. It was stuck. An old man who happened by tried to help him get back on the pavement, but the right rear tire just sank deeper.

After another two hours, Krauss could hardly believe his eyes. A young Arab was riding on some contraption made from the empty shell of an old car. The front fenders had been removed, the hood was gone, and the engine and radiator were missing. The car's empty shell was being drawn by two old, run-down horses. They were pulling the vehicle like a cart, with the driver sitting on the cowl in front of the missing windshield. It was a sight Krauss would never forget. When he waved it down, he found the young man did not speak German or English. He mimed hooking one of the animals up to the rear bumper and pulling it out. The Arab understood and tied one of the horses to it.

Soon, the car was cleared enough for Krauss to get traction again. Searching his pockets, he found a crumpled-up dollar bill. The young Arab seemed happy to receive it. Krauss estimated he had another forty kilometers before he was near any Germans. He remembered from the briefing he had to keep the mountains to his right.

The gas gauge was almost empty, so he started looking for some way to get more precious fuel. He found a village with a peddler's stand that had one-gallon containers of fuel. He had no money, but he did have a Bulova he'd bought at the Fort Benning PX as a graduation reminder. The seller, speaking a little German, agreed to trade two gallons for Krauss's watch. Krauss pointed to a used shirt and got that thrown in. On the move again, he hoped he might get another forty kilometers before he again ran out of gas.

After ten hours, he came to the top of another dune and started down the other side. Suddenly, a rifle cracked. The impact of a bullet coming through the driver's side door knocked him to the side of the seat. He tried to grab the steering wheel to stop his slide. Through the right window, he saw a German soldier aiming his Mauser at his head. "You shot me! You son of a sow! I'm a German officer!" Krauss shouted.

The soldier rushed the last few steps and prepared to fire again. Krauss shouted, *"Nein!* I am German. A Luftwaffe officer!"

The soldier motioned him out of the car. He crawled out with difficulty, bleeding. As other soldiers ran toward them, he collapsed.

The squad members carried him to the nearest aid station, where a field doctor tended his wounds. He told his story of being a Luftwaffe officer on a special mission for Reichsmarschall Goring. They sent him under guard to unit headquarters, where a colonel questioned him.

"I am Luftwaffe Lieutenant Werner Krauss, serial number 543-86-77. Contact the Reichsmarschall's office or his secretary, Sergeant Reicher. They will confirm this."

The Colonel seemed inclined to believe him but still guarded him until Berlin could confirm his story. He allowed him to eat, have another doctor look at his wounds, and get some rest.

The next day, after radio confirmation of his identity, the colonel gave him an army field uniform and called Rommel about what to do with him.

Rommel said, "Any need to further debrief him?"

The colonel answered, "Krauss knows about U.S. Army basic training, parachute training, and the American landing that's already happened. If you want to know anything about his original mission, you'd have to deal with the Reichsmarschall."

"Have a doctor recheck him, then put him on a plane to Tunis. We still control it but must soon move back from our position here. Once there, get him on a boat or plane back to Berlin."

"Jawohl, Herr Feldmarschall," said the colonel.

BERLIN
SEPTEMBER 20, 1942

In Berlin, Krauss went directly to the Air Ministry. Not having identification, he was almost arrested by the guards. He pointed to his wounds and pleaded with the desk to call Reicher to identify him.

When Reicher arrived, she recognized him. "Captain Krauss, we thought you'd been captured and executed." She noted his bandages and sling. "Are you in pain?"

"I'm healing. It's a long story, Sergeant. I'll happily review the entire mission with you or the Reichsmarschall."

"Certainly, Captain. Oh, and congratulations on your promotion."

On the way to the Reichsmarschall's, Krauss asked about Gunther and Muller. The sergeant said, "They were both promoted after the presentation of the Mona Lisa to der Fuhrer. You were promoted posthumously, or so they thought. Gunther was reassigned to Operations and Plans, and Muller is with Abwehr counterintelligence now."

"I heard on the way home we're having a rough time on the Eastern Front?"

In thought for a moment, Reicher finally said, "That's not my place to comment on, Captain."

"If the General's not in, can you get me a Luftwaffe uniform and proper identification?"

"Certainly. You can use Major Gunther's old office until the General returns. I have your sizes from when we ordered the clothes for the team."

"I noticed you aren't wearing a wedding ring, Sergeant. Are you married?"

"My husband was killed in Poland, Captain."

"I'm sorry to hear that. Forgive me for being forward, but would you consider dinner some evening?"

"I'm not sure that would be appropriate, Captain."

"It is appropriate, and you'll be above reproach, Sergeant."

She hesitated, but finally smiled. "All right, I'd like that, Captain."

"Please call me Werner. As you might expect, I'm exhausted. We'll pick an evening once I'm rested. Thank you for your assistance."

In Gunther's office, he was so tired he fell asleep at the table. He was awakened three hours later when an enlisted man delivered a captain's uniform. "Sir, your ID will have to wait until tomorrow. The Marshal will return then."

Krauss cleaned up and changed, then went to the mess for pork knuckle, cabbage, and potato dumplings. He thought *I haven't eaten this well since parachute school.*

The next day, he told Goring the long story of how he'd volunteered for the U.S. Army to keep with his cover of being a college student. He also told him how he'd wound up in the emergency room, paired with an army recruiter. He told of his initial plan to escape into the United States after basic training until he heard of the operation to drop parachutists into North Africa. Then, of his escape and being shot by their own troops.

Goring was fascinated. Of course, he wanted to have Propaganda Minister Goebbels tell Krauss's story about putting one over on the Americans, though without mentioning the *Mona Lisa.*

"And where would you like to be stationed now?"

"If possible, Sir, I'd like to be on the Marshal's staff."

"Consider it done, Captain, and add a wound badge and Iron Cross 2nd class to your other decorations."

"Yes, sir!"

EIGHTEEN

WASHINGTON
OCTOBER 5, 1942

Having taken a long weekend off from his Biltmore duties, Daniel had driven the four hundred and eighty miles to Washington. He'd considered taking a train, but that would have added a day. He needed to return to North Carolina this evening. It would be a miracle if he didn't fall asleep at the wheel on the return trip. *It would be perfect if we had roads like the Autobahn or more Pennsylvania Turnpikes.*

He arrived at Wellington's with the senator's new Mona Lisa. *The old Chevy is on its last legs,* he thought. *Heck, I can buy a new car when they become available. Maybe a Lincoln.*

He felt sure the painting was as close to the Louvre's as anyone other than Leonardo could make it.

When the maid ushered him into the study, the senator was already into the scotch and waiting.

Daniel carefully unwrapped the trophy and placed her on the easel the Senator had already set up.

Wellington looked excited as he leaned in to see the details. He walked around the easel to look at all sides of the painting. He opened his desk drawer and pulled out a magnifying glass. He studied the frame, spending a little extra time in the lower right-hand corner. *Must be where he marked his original frame,* Daniel thought.

Wellington then looked hard at the painting, going very slowly. He spent time with the lens, looking at the rear of the panel. He lingered at the large "9" drawn on the reverse. *And, where he marked the original painting,* thought Daniel.

He turned the painting around on the easel and stepped back.

"Is it truly she?" Wellington asked, almost as if Daniel were not in the room.

"It is, Senator. A long journey, but now she is yours."

The old man sat down heavily. He looked happily exhausted. "Marvelous!" He sighed. "Scotch, Daniel?"

"I'd better not, Senator. I've got to drive back."

"This is my top-shelf, special occasion whiskey, Daniel."

"Certainly, Senator. One finger, one cube, please."

Wellington poured from his bottle of The Dalmore 20-year single malt.

Daniel sipped his. "This is very smooth, Senator. Do I taste sherry?"

"From the final cask. I knew you'd like it. Tell me, what was the hardest part of the job?"

"There were two main challenges. Getting time alone with the paintings in the Living Hall and opening Donahue's puzzle crate. It took me three dozen attempts. I needed an unbelievable three hours to open it, switch the frames, and reassemble it. I had to hide the Mona Lisa behind crates of other paintings. I did not have time to take her to my room before I was to be relieved. I had to move her the following evening and was almost discovered."

"Well, you've done it, Danny. After I get her authenticated, I'll move the money to your account."

Stunned but not showing it, Daniel said, "Do you think that's necessary, Senator? Antoine Buchard and I have both authenticated her. Wouldn't you think that's already two of the world's leading authorities on da Vinci's works?"

Wellington drained his scotch and stared at Daniel for several seconds. Finally, he said, "Do you want the two million in the same account where you received the advance?"

Again, employing his poker face, Daniel said, "That would be fine, Senator."

"It will be done tomorrow. You've made my wish come true."

"It would be nice if you could share her with the world. It's a shame that can never happen."

"She, you, and I will know," said the Senator. "Is there anything else, Daniel?"

"I could use some gas coupons, Senator; I have a lot of driving to do."

"I have some here." He opened one of his desk drawers.

An hour later, after discussing other valuable artworks, Daniel said goodbye and left the Senator as he toasted the lady.

That, he thought, as he walked down the steps of the house, *almost turned dicey. He's suspicious. What will I do if the money doesn't show? I need to leave some documentation in case something happens to me. I wouldn't rule it out with a guy this power-hungry and having friends like the Hoff gang. Hell, he could* save two million by having me whacked, and it'd probably cost him a hundred bucks or less. It's a good thing for me Biltmore has great security.

BILTMORE
NOVEMBER 17, 1942

Back at the Estate, Daniel got a call from R. J. Rogers. "Daniel, you've done an excellent job at the Biltmore, but you need a rest after being there for over a year. I've decided to send Eugene Jenkins to relieve you. He'll be there next Tuesday."

"Thanks, Ray! I'd love to get back to the museum."

That evening, Daniel went into town and closed out his room at Dot's.

Three days later, he showed Eugene Jenkins the house and introduced him to Mr. Cecil, Antoine, Phillipe, the other Frenchmen, and Donahue.

* * *

Daniel made a second pass of the house and said goodbye to Mr. Cecil, Buchard, and the other Frenchmen.

As he stepped into the Chevrolet, he thought, *Goodbye, grand estate, my war story will be different from most. Who will believe the Mona Lisa herself once graced Biltmore House?*

EIGHTEEN MONTHS LATER

BILTMORE
JUNE 15, 1944

The Allies had landed and were driving East through France. Any German assault on the U.S. was out of the question now. The directors at the National Gallery wanted their works returned to D.C.

Eugene Jenkins and Antoine Buchard had been instructed by R.J. Rogers to be ready to move everything within the next 72 hours.

As Jenkins and Buchard checked the crates against the inventory from when they'd moved in, Buchard said, "Will you be taking the puzzle crate to the Gallery?"

"I didn't think about it," said Jenkins. "What are your thoughts?"

"It is worthy of display somewhere. Perhaps at the Gallery, with signage telling how it helped keep France's national treasure, The Mona Lisa, safe during the war."

"That's a great idea, Antoine. I'll call Ray Rogers and run it by him."

Rogers also felt it was a great idea and told Jenkins to load it along with all the other pieces.

* * *

Antoine had invited Jenkins to watch as he removed the *Mona Lisa* from the crate. "You'll need to know how to open this when you control it."

After Jenkins had watched them open it and transfer the painting to a regular crate, Buchard had him open and then reassemble the box twice for practice. Jenkins had taken notes.

Buchard and Jenkins then went to say their goodbyes to Mr. Cecil, who asked, "Any idea when you'll get to return to Paris?"

"Best estimates seem to suggest eight to twelve months. Maybe sooner, depending on the carnage left after the Allies take control of the city."

"Let's hope it's sooner," said Cecil.

Continuing to Donahue's office, they chatted with the army men for a few moments, then wished them a quick end to the war. Having loaded all the artworks onto the vans, Buchard, Jenkins, and the Frenchmen got into their automobile, along with the *Mona Lisa*, and prepared to escort the vans to Washington. They were followed by two North Carolina Highway Patrol cars.

* * *

In his office, Donahue was on the line with Colonel Powell. "Good morning, Captain. I hear the paintings are leaving for D.C."

"Correct, Colonel, they just pulled out."

"So, your assignment there is over. My base provost marshal is being promoted and transferred to Fort Bragg. Would you be interested in being my provost marshal here at Morris? You'd be in charge of a company of MPs and overall base security."

"Wilco, Colonel. Yes, I'm interested."

"If you wish, you can bring up to five of your current team as MPs. The others will be merged into maintenance. Since this war began, Morris has seen our headcount increase by three hundred percent. The provost billet calls for a major to oversee security, so you'll be promoted effective with the receipt of your orders."

"Looking forward to the job, sir."

"Not to put a damper on anyone's career, Declan, but I believe the war in Europe will be over in less than a year. We'll have licked the Hun again by then. The Pacific will be tougher. After we finish both theaters, the Army will return to peacetime levels. So, in two years, most of us will be looking at retiring. Just giving you a heads-up. It may impact your twenty."

"Solid insight, Colonel. I'll look for my orders."

"They'll be there by tomorrow. See you in 48 hours."

"Roger that, Colonel."

He went to his office and found Gibbs at his desk. He gave Gibbs an overview of what would be happening and asked him to call the men together.

"Also, dismantle the temporary sentry stands and pile the wood outside the carpenter's shop. Tear down the bunk beds and load them. You can discontinue the sentry posts."

After the men assembled in the stable's courtyard, Donahue said, "Our job here's complete. We'll be heading to Morris. Some of you will be MPs, and others will go into maintenance duties. Thank you for the job you've done here in the last thirty months. Any questions?"

Private Ballard said, "Any chance we'll wind up in the Pacific, Captain? See some action at last."

"I can't say for sure, above my paygrade. Ask Hirohito. Our transportation will be here in the next forty-eight hours. Everyone who wants it will get a week's leave once we check into Morris. Any other questions?" He turned to Gibbs. "Dismiss the men, Sergeant."

"Fall out and police the grounds," said the sergeant.

Donahue also went by the carpenter's shop. "Thanks for your work on the puzzle box. It was a big success and was well-received by many who saw it. It will one day be on exhibit at the National Gallery, and you'll be credited for creating it. Well done, Joseph."

Joseph grinned under his huge mustache as he shook Donahue's hand.

BILTMORE
JUNE 17, 1944

Two days later, finding Mr. Cecil in the library, Donahue thanked him. "I hope to see you under different circumstances in the future. Thank you for supporting this very different kind of mission."

"My pleasure, Major, and congratulations on your promotion."

Leaving the library, Donahue went to find Randolph and thanked him for his assistance.

He walked around to the South Terrace and surveyed the gardens. He'd come to feel comforted in their orderly beauty over the last two and a half years.

Returning to the office, he said, "The trucks are here; load 'em up." As they pulled out, Gibbs jumped into the Morris Field jeep they'd been using and followed.

Donahue took one last look around, placed his propeller in the back seat, climbed into his car, and followed the convoy. He felt that the previous three years of his life would be a great story for his grandchildren someday.

If Alaina was willing, of course.

NINETEEN

SAUSALITO, CALIFORNIA
OCTOBER 3, 1945

Daniel Roberts's Northern Gate Gallery was holding its Grand Opening in the up-and-coming community of Sausalito, just across the Bay from the metropolis of San Francisco. Champagne and hors d'oeuvres were piled high on silver settings. He recognized art critics from San Francisco, Los Angeles, and one who he believed was from New York City.

He'd spent four hundred thousand dollars purchasing his first collection to display for sale. He was very proud of the presentation, which included the custom *Mona Lisa*-style frame from the 1500s.

Daniel chatted with Wiley Poole from the *Los Angeles Times*, Kenneth Davis from the *San Francisco Examiner*, and several lesser-known critics.

The opening had been in progress for three hours, and he was exhausted. He was ready to retire to his apartment above the gallery. He told his assistant, Jason, he would go upstairs for a bit.

"Go on, sir. I can handle this. It's mostly free-loaders who are left."

He heard a familiar voice as he turned to start up the partially hidden stairs. "Daniel, congratulations!"

He turned to see Antoine Buchard. Poole and Davis were trying to get Buchard's attention. Antoine said, waving them both away, "Please. I'm visiting a friend from our days at the Biltmore."

The critics reluctantly retreated to the champagne table.

"Antoine! How very kind of you to stop by my humble gallery."

"I was in Washington for a formal thank you from my government to yours. I heard of your opening and decided to fly out. I wish you success."

"Would you like a personal tour?"

"I would. We can talk about our time at the Biltmore together."

* * *

Daniel showed Antoine a lovely early-period Renoir and a lower-end Matisse.

When they came to the *Mona Lisa*-style frame, Antoine stopped and intently studied it. The lights Daniel had installed to highlight it made detailed inspection easy. After a while, Antoine simply nodded.

As they stood together, and with no one else around, the Frenchman said, in a low voice, while still staring at the frame, "I don't know who your buyer was, but I hope you intended to swindle him. The switch with the copy in my room had to mean the buyer had supplied you with another Chaudron. No harm, really. All six are of equal value. Best of luck with your gallery, Daniel. Be sure to stop by the Louvre if you get to Paris again."

After a stunned moment and once again employing his poker face, Daniel said, "France should give you a medal for your efforts in safekeeping their national treasure."

If you and they only knew, thought Buchard.

"Mind if I ask you one thing, Antoine?"

"What's that?"

"What was the secret to Donahue's puzzle box?"

Antoine smiled. "Magnets. More European than Oriental. It likely was the carpenter's idea."

Daniel shook his head, then nodded as if in agreement.

"Goodbye." Buchard turned and walked out.

Daniel didn't know what had just transpired, but it felt like approval had just been issued. Slipping his hand into his left pocket, he rubbed his lucky nickel.

TWENTY

THE LOUVRE
PARIS
NOVEMBER 30, 1945

President Charles de Gaulle presented France's National Order of the *Legion d'Honneur (Chevalier)* to Antoine Buchard, assistant Phillipe Jourdan, and policemen Maurice Caron and Jules Mathieu.

The citations read:

> *For outstanding performance of duty while safeguarding France's most valued treasure, Leonardo da Vinci's* La Jaconde *painting, from March 9, 1939, through June 3, 1945.*

As de Gaulle pinned the award to Antoine's suit coat lapel, he said, "Well done, Antoine. The National Gallery personnel and the army major were very impressed with your service during your time in America. You received a very flattering endorsement from the U.S. National Gallery's Daniel Roberts."

The President then pinned the award to the chests of the other three men.

The authentic *Mona Lisa* sat in splendor on an easel beside the four men.

EPILOGUE

THE FATE OF THE *MONA LISAS* AND THE CHARACTERS IN THIS NOVEL:

Mona Lisa #1: This Yves Chaudron replica was returned to the Louvre in 1913 and was believed to be the original *Mona Lisa* for twenty-eight years. It was displayed at the 1939 World's Fair and then at the National Gallery until it was transferred to Biltmore. It was switched from the puzzle crate to Buchard's room. Daniel Roberts then switched it for Wellington's Chaudron copy and placed it in Bobby Sledge's replica frame. Delivered to Senator Wellington, he continued to believe it to be the real *Mona Lisa*. Wellington's surviving family, using updated authentication techniques, determined it to be a copy in 1960. It was sold to a Japanese private collector in 1962.

Mona Lisa #2: Hermann Goring purchased this painting in France in 1920. In 1941, it was delivered by U-boat to the U.S., where Gunther switched it for *Mona Lisa #3*, the Louvre's donated Chaudron copy. An inspection by Antoine Buchard revealed this painting to be the authentic da Vinci *Mona Lisa*. It is on display at the Louvre today.

Mona Lisa #3: This Chaudron was donated by a private collector to the Louvre in 1922. It was the museum's official backup copy for those few times the *Mona Lisa* was on display outside the Louvre. Bouchard switched it from the puzzle crate with *Mona Lisa* #1. The Germans switched it for *Mona Lisa* #2, the Goring Chaudron copy. *Mona Lisa* #3 was presented to Adolf Hitler. After the war, she was recovered by "The Monuments Men" and is back in the Louvre today as a second example of Chaudron's replicas.

Mona Lisa #4: This is the Chaudron Senator Wellington horse-traded for in France in 1917. It was switched for the Louvre's donated Chaudron copy, *Mona Lisa* #1, by Daniel Roberts at the Biltmore. It is now the Louvre's backup copy at the museum, having replaced *Mona Lisa* #3.

Rumors exist that a Chaudron copy is in a private collection in Uruguay, but the true whereabouts of the other three Chaudron *Mona Lisas* remain unknown. No mention was ever made about a copy being returned to the Louvre in 1914.

Antoine Buchard became the director of the Louvre in 1956. He never told the full story of the *Mona Lisa's* journey and never remarried. He made frequent trips to the United States to lecture on art restoration but never met with Daniel Roberts again.

Sergeant Walter Hellwig refused repatriation to Germany and received asylum in the U.S. He married, had two sons, and lived out his life in the hills of Tennessee, where he eventually purchased Tom Teas's Dairy Farm. In 1952, he became a naturalized United States citizen and formally changed his name to Christopher Wagg.

Rolf Gunther escaped to Argentina during the final defense of Berlin in April 1945. He settled in Neuquen, Argentina, where he became an avid trout fisherman and later a fishing guide in Tierra del Fuego. He married into a wealthy Argentinian family.

Declan Donahue and Alaina Avara were married in 1946 and had one child, a girl. They live in Charlotte, North Carolina. Donahue retired from the Army in 1955. Declan and Alaina's daughter, Danica, joined the Air Force and eventually became one of the first female astronauts.

Werner Krauss and Sergeant Reicher, after getting together, died in the final battle between Russian forces and Berlin's last defenders.

Conrad Muller lived through Berlin's final defense. He was not prosecuted for any war crimes and escaped to West Berlin, where he worked as an art restoration technician. He married and had three children.

Lillian Jagemann lost her gallery and her husband. Her part in the Goring plan was never discovered. She moved to Chicago, Illinois, and started an art gallery on North Michigan Avenue. She and her three cats live alone.

Daniel Roberts continued to run the very successful Northern Gate Gallery in Sausalito. In 1949, his "antique" frame sold for $45,000. Daniel adopted twin girls. He lived in Sausalito until his death from natural causes in 1982. His daughters made sure he was buried with his lucky nickel.

Senator Archibald Wellington died in 1966. His son discovered a hidden room in their home in Maine, and, where possible, the art pieces were anonymously returned to their rightful owners. At that time, Wellington's *Mona Lisa* #4 was tested and proven to be a forgery. Believed to be another Chaudron replica, it is stored in the National Gallery.

Master Sergeant Buford Willie Gibbs returned to Bowling Green, Kentucky. He was elected mayor of Bowling Green in 1948. He spearheaded the construction of a WWI and WWII memorial at the local veteran's cemetery. Gibbs died from cancer in 1954.

Adolf Hitler committed suicide in his bunker on April 30, 1945.

Hermann Goring committed suicide on October 15, 1946, during his War Crimes trial in Nuremberg, Germany.

Elise Schneider married a television producer in 1950 and lived in Santa Monica. She had no children and never talked about her years at Biltmore House. She lived to be 100 years old. She never met Errol Flynn.

ACKNOWLEDGEMENTS

Betty Thomas Smith - I could not have written this book without my retired teacher spouse's support and editing skills. She edited every pass of each chapter, even after I had passed it through Grammarly's software. She made the book much better.

David Poyer - Editor extraordinaire, friend, and fellow Navy man, made this book much better.

Daniel D. Smith, Jr. - Counting my four military history reference books, Daniel has created five book jackets for me. They have all been outstanding and have greatly helped sell the books.

Beta Readers – Keith Edward Vaughn, Sarah P. Webb, Will Rowe, Mary Lewis, Eric Jonassen, Betty Thomas Smith, Charles Carter, Daniel D. Smith, Jr., Angela Smith Ballard and Michael S. Ballard

"Hat tip" to Karl Decker, who presented the possibility of Yves Chaudron and his remarkable Mona Lisa replicas. The intrigue continues.

"Hat tip" to Andy Schoneberg for his work in painting an exact replica of the Mona Lisa and finishing/aging/distressing an exact copy of the frame. Andy documented his whole process.

ABOUT THE AUTHOR

Photo: Betty Thomas Smith

Daniel D. Smith Sr. is a military historian. He served 26 years in the Navy, retiring as a command senior chief. After retirement, he joined the all-volunteer Tennessee State Guard as an Infantry Captain. After seven years in the State Guard, he retired as a Lieutenant Colonel.

In a second career, he retired from the Tennessee Valley Authority as an IT Manager.

From 1997 to 1999, Smith was executive director of the National Medal of Honor Museum of Military History in Chattanooga, Tennessee.

He has published four military history reference books, many classic car magazine articles, and short fiction pieces. This is his first novel.

Aside from reading, Smith's favorite pastime is showing and judging classic automobiles. He and his wife, Betty, have two adult children and live in Chattanooga, Tennessee.

Visit at: DanielSmithBooks.net

The Medal of Honor and the Battles for Chattanooga

Author: Daniel D. Smith, Sr.
ISBN: 979-8-9905843-3-4
Copyright: 2013
Pages: 64, (75 b&w photographs)
Size: 8.5 x 11 in., Perfect Bound

U.S. Navy Tailor-Made Dress Blues, Liberty Cuffs, and Sailor Folk Art

Author: Daniel D. Smith, Sr.
ISBN: 979-8-9905843-2-7
Copyright: 2010
Pages: 104, (145 color photographs)
Size: 8.5 x 11 in., Perfect Bound

U.S. Navy Memorabilia: Web Belt Buckles, Unit Plaques, Lighters & Ashtrays

Author: Daniel D. Smith, Sr.
ISBN: 979-8-9905843-4-1
Copyright: 2012
Pages: 104, (200 color photographs)
Size: 8.5 x 11 in., Perfect Bound

The U.S. Navy's Use of Law Enforcement-Style Badges

Author: Daniel D. Smith, Sr.
ISBN: 978-0-692-64374-7
Copyright: 2016
Pages: 89, (hundreds of color photographs)
Size: 8.5 x 11 in., Perfect Bound

Your reviews help indie authors get noticed. If you enjoyed this book, please leave a review at Amazon.com or GoodReads.com. I hope you enjoyed this work, and thank you for reading. Daniel D. Smith, Sr.

Amazon Review   Goodreads Review